the best of all possible worlds,
or the depths of Hell?

I heard something and turned onto my back and looked to the doorway. I saw only the pink of her nightgown and the white of her smile.

"Can I sleep with you?"

I didn't answer. I simply didn't believe the dream. She came out of the faint back-lighting of the hallway, into the shadowed room. Close to the bed. Now lifting a corner of sheet and blanket, her voice so soft and breathy, she asked again, "Can I sleep with you?"

The wine-hot corpuscles were surging so strongly all witticisms fled in the face of a swallowed, "Yes." She came into my bed, knees up, covers up, legs straightening and shifting and finding her comfortable hold on me as if we had slept together a hundred times. Familiar and relaxed and hot. "Goddamn," I breathed, "you're a lot of woman, Julie."

I was a rock in a minute. Her eyes and smile luminescent in the dimness, she sighed as she took me inside with her soft hand and pulled my head to her mouth. Afterward, she laid her hot cheek on my chest and told me she loved me. Honestly and with feeling. She meant it.

Perhaps she meant it then—that moment, that night. But how could he trust her, trust anyone in that California Eden where a man could have anything in the world he wanted—except his freedom, and the right to think? . . .

P.J. O'Shaughnessy

TRAUMA

PINNACLE BOOKS • LOS ANGELES

TRAUMA

Copyright © 1978 by P. J. O'Shaughnessy

An original Pinnacle Books edition,
published for the first time anywhere.

First printing, October 1978

ISBN: 0-523-40359-3

Cover illustration by Paul Stinson

Printed in the United States of America

PINNACLE BOOKS, INC.
2029 Century Park East
Los Angeles, California 90067

For my mother and father

Diseases desperate grown
By desperate appliance are reliev'd,
Or not at all.

Hamlet, Act Four

Special thanks to Dr. Fred Shima,
Associate Professor of Psychology at the
University of California

1.

THE knuckles of my hand are stiff.

I must drop the pencil occasionally and rub them warm. All the bones of my body ache dully and it occurs to me that even the dread of death is a subjectively relative thing, welcomed as often as not by the poor and ailing while the rich and pleasured tremble at its mention.

The thought brings a smile to my dry lips. But the smile fades as I once again face the vacant page with a resharpened pencil. The yellow legal pad is ragged at the top testifying to the ripped out pages of a dozen aborted beginnings.

The problem is that there is no beginning. Not a concrete fixed point in time labeled with fixed dated events to proceed from.

So I must put it down as one narrates a dream, picking up at a point whose only qualification is that it is a clearly remembered moment, and then relate from there.

The story is a dream turned nightmare, so I will begin with the dream within the dream, that I still remember. . .

A face.

An old woman's face. Powder white and wrinkled, cast in a blue sourceless light. Crow black, incongruously healthy hair framed the face enormous in my mind's eye.

The thin slash of red that was her mouth parted to reveal the too-perfect teeth of dentures. A voice filtered through a loudspeaker and ordered me to stand up.

Below the woman's face there appeared a hand incredibly old, the skin so thin the flow of blood was visible in the sculptured veins.

"What do you see?" a remote electronic voice asked.

"She wants me to take her hand," I said.

"Then take it, Sebby," the voice crackled.

"I want to sleep," I said and sank back down on the cot.

"No!" the voice ordered, "take her hand!"

I sat back up and reached my hand out to hers and with a shudder of pure terror I saw my hand pass through hers.

She wasn't real.

The enormous face loomed larger and she

2

smiled a broad smile that bared the false pink gums above the false white teeth.

Just before I passed out I heard a voice say: "One more day in the D.C. lab and we'll have the key. One more day."

2.

I don't know how long I had slept. When I awakened, a nurse was chastising me.

"Sebastian," she said, "I am not angry with you, but this is the fourth time you have wet your bed. We have to change the sheets each time. You can understand how that's annoying, can't you?"

"I'm sorry," I said.

A young man in a white uniform, who I wrongly presumed was a doctor, suddenly appeared behind the nurse and advised her that he would relieve her of me.

"Relax, Mr. Cant, you're fine now. My name is John," he said very pleasantly. "You're all right now." Then, quietly, "Do you want to stay here?"

I cocked my head, puzzled.

He began tucking in my sheet, which didn't need tucking, and he continued in a subdued tone with as little lip movement as possible. "Just do as you are told," he urged. "Say as little as possible or nothing at all."

"Why?" I asked.

"There!" he said aloud and perfunctorily brushed away a few remaining creases in the top sheet. A tall nurse walked up to my bed and greeted the orderly with: "How is he, John?" Then to me: "How are you, Mr. Cant?" She had Irish black hair and eyes of the lightest blue possible. She was beautiful.

"This is Miss Goldberg."

I just lay there and looked in her beautiful eyes while she punctured my arm with a hypodermic. The warm sun filled the room and highlighted her hair and in a moment I was asleep.

When I awoke, a black nurse I hadn't seen before was approaching me. I could just make her out in the dim light. Just as quickly another nurse appeared beside her, and they both looked at me intently. I felt dizzy and passed out.

"Wake up, Sebastian, you've done it again." It was the black nurse.

"I'm sorry."

The two nurses rolled me over, folded the undersheet in half, rolled me back again, removed the wet sheet, and reversed the process with a new sheet.

"Hold the handle of the bottle like this and

with your other hand place your penis in the bottle like this."

"Hey, let go of my dick!"

"I'm a nurse."

"I don't care," I told her, "don't just grab my dick like that! That's my dick!"

"I was just trying to explain . . ."

"I know how," I interrupted.

"Mr. Cant, you must try to control yourself. It's very important that you urinate."

"Where's the fire?" I said and began laughing hysterically as if I had just told the funniest joke in the world.

At the far end of the room, barely visible, I could make out the orderly, John, and Miss Goldberg. They were staring at me intently. John marched over to me and his face wore a frown but he said nothing.

"I'm sorry," I said, without the vaguest notion of what I was apologizing for.

"Never mind; lie still. I have to give you some medication. Just trust me, Sebastian."

"Okay," I assured him and he jabbed me with a hypodermic. I drew the sheet up and settled on my back. Miss Goldberg appeared.

"When will I find out what's going on?" I asked, and uncontrollable tears blurred my eyes.

"Soon," she said, "pretty soon."

"I'm scared, Miss Goldberg, really scared. I don't know why I'm here. I don't know how long . . . I don't remember anything. Do I have amnesia? Is that it?"

"Not exactly, Sebastian, but you are supposed to try to remember everything you can."

I lay weeping and once again slipped into a drug-induced sleep.

3.

"HOW are you feeling, Mr. Cant?"

"Groggy," I answered, still not awake.

There was no reply to my comment and as my eyes cleared I saw Miss Goldberg at the foot of the bed armed with a hypodermic. I turned my gaze to the right and saw the source of the voice that awakened me. It was an expensive maroon jacket, white shirt, and white tie on a handsome man in his late forties, or early fifties, gray at the temples, and not particularly tall or bulky but exuding a quiet strength and power.

It was still daylight, barely, and I could see I was still in the room, with the beautiful view of the mountains.

"Hold my hand," he said. I obeyed. "Now squeeze as hard as you can." I squeezed. "Good," he said. "Very good."

8

"What the hell is going on?" I pleaded help-lessly.

"You and I are going to have a long talk, Sebastian."

"That's fine with me. I'd like a long talk. I'd like some explanations."

"We will have that long talk. Not now, but very soon, Sebastian."

He moved to the foot of the bed, removed my chart, wrote something on it, and, placing his pen back in his shirt pocket, he repeated, "Very soon." And started toward the door.

"Doc!" He turned and faced me. "Doc," I said with urgency and no apparent reason, "I'll tell you everything, everything I can remember."

He nodded, smiled, turned, and left. Miss Goldberg and needle advanced.

"On your stomach, Mr. Cant," she ordered.

I rolled over submissively, resting my chin on the back of my hand. "Where am I?"

"You are at Sunnyview Hospital, Mr. Cant."

"Who was that doctor?"

"That," she said as she annointed my but-tocks, "is Doctor Manna."

"Who?"

"Manna," she repeated, accompanying the name with the stabbing. "He's head of the hos-pital." She erased the puncture with alcohol-dampened cotton and I rolled on my back as she brought up the sheets.

9

"Doctor Manna would like you to read this." She produced a small blue hardcover book from the slit pocket of her uniform and with a wish for a pleasant night's sleep turned and left the room. As the door closed softly behind her, I read the red-lettered title. It was Orwell's *1984* and my mind reeled with fearful imaginings before the drugs closed my lids in sleep.

Once again I awoke, slipping into a whirlpool of hysteria because of the alien environment that greeted my eyes. The panic was stemmed by the sight and sound of Miss Goldberg, who was standing bedside.

"How about a little sunshine?" she asked brightly. And stretching over a chair on her long beautiful legs, she pulled a cord that opened the drapes to a vista of rolling brown hills tinted pink with a blooming dawn.

"Isn't it beautiful!" she said to the hills.

"Yes," I said, "it is pretty."

She came over to my bed and put an arm on either side of my head to fluff my pillow.

I'm sure my expression approximated the look of a month-old calf.

She stopped her motions with the pillow, but was still leaning over me. Her perfume was making me dizzy.

She brought her face close and kissed me lightly on the lips.

"I have to give you a shot, Sebastian."

"You may kill me, Miss Goldberg, if that is your whim."

She drew down the sheet.

"Over we go," she said and then tightening her voice slightly in concentration, "why don't you call me Julie?"

"Julie. That's a pretty name."

"Thank you." She swabbed the target with cotton. Squeeze. Jab. Wipe. She drew the sheets up and began tucking them in. "Dr. Manna will be seeing you this morning. In his office."

"Good. Will you be here when I get back?"

She finished and straightened up. "I'll be here." She smiled and started for the door.

"Julie?" She turned, still smiling. "Will that shot . . . will it put me back to sleep?"

I think she knew that implicit in the question was the more subtle question, "Can I trust you?"

"No, Sebastian, the opposite. It will wake you up."

She left the room. I rolled over to face the hills and mountains yellowing warmly in the morning sun and actually heard birds singing.

As I lay there in contentment it seemed that things were becoming clearer moment to moment. I was in a room about twenty feet square; one wall, except for the bottom three or four feet, was all glass, framing a very real landscape of nearby hills and distant mountains

11

with peaks of snow here and there. The hills were soft-shouldered brown California hills. Plump giants sleeping under khaki army blankets. The room was occupied by only one other patient, an old man fast asleep. He was so thin and jaundiced that only a slight rise and fall of his chest assured me that he was alive.

The door opened and I turned to see a nurse squeaking a wheelchair toward me, maneuvering it alongside my bed. They don't even look like wheelchairs anymore, I mused. Not the marvelous creaky wood chairs that Lionel Barrymore used to grunt around in. These modern jobs with their blue plastic handgrips look for the world like mutated bicycles.

The nurse at the helm was young, very young, with long straight blonde hair, and so pretty to be plain—the kind who, upon seeing the Roman Coliseum, the Taj Mahal, or the Cathedral of Notre Dame, would comment profoundly, "Far out."

"We're going to take a little trip, Mr. Cant," she announced as she pulled back the sheets and began helping me out of bed. "My name is Debbi."

"What else?" I mumbled.

"Pardon me?"

"Nothing, Deborah." I was easing myself out of bed and realizing how bloody stiff my joints were.

"It's just spelled D-e-b-b-i."

12

"Not i-e?"

"No, my mother wanted it to be different."

"An imaginative woman."

"Pardon me?" she said.

I eased myself into the mobile lawn chair. My arms were still strong, but my legs were ready for Social Security.

"Comfortable, Mr. Cant?"

"Comfortable as a whore at high mass."

"As what? Oh, I get it. Far out!"

Debbi-with-an-"i" opened the door and clicked the rubber stop down to hold it ajar. She then retrieved me and we were on our way to God knew where. We made a hard right at the nurses' station, and at the next intersection almost had a successful head-on with a gurney being wheeled by two men in green gowns and caps. There was a woman on the gurney, face up, eyes closed, and very still

"Where are they taking her, Debbi?"

"I don't know. Maybe they're going to operate on her, maybe."

"What makes you say that?"

"I don't know. That was surgery they wheeled her into so I guess they're going to operate."

"Far out."

"Pardon me?"

I wondered vaguely how heavy might be the responsibilities entrusted to Debbi-with-an-"i." My imagination conjured up a scarifying picture of mineself on an operating table with Debbi as chief assistant to the surgeon, snapping bubble gum and admiring her reflection in the console that monitored my vital life signs.

"Pardon me, Mr. Cant," said Debbi as she parked me at one side of the hall, clicked a brake, stepped over to a door, knocked, and entered. In a moment she reappeared.

"What room is that, Debbi?"

"That's Dr. Manna's office. He wants to see you."

"Now?"

"No, not now." Obviously—we were again in second gear and continuing onward. "He wants you to sit out on the patio and have lunch and relax for a while."

"That's just what I need. Rest."

"Pardon me?"

"I said, far out."

"Yeah."

Parked on the terrace, I could truly appreciate why they named the place Sunnyview. There were the mountains and hills again, only from the terrace the scene was panoramic. It struck me that though I could see for miles, I saw no sign of civilization beyond the hospital grounds. I guessed that I was on the third or fourth floor.

The beautiful Miss Goldberg was right, I reflected. The last medication injected into my patient long-suffering ass was indeed not a sleep inducer. I had been feeling good, even humorous, the last few waking hours, and I wondered if it was because I seemed to be awake, really awake for the first time in memory. I sat for some time soaking up the warm sun and almost dozed into a natural sleep that was aborted by the clattering of one of those busboy-type aluminum carts zeroing in on me around tables and chairs, guided by a candystriper. A really lovely name for those young, pretty little just-graduated-from-high-school girls who work in hospitals. Little Flo Nightingales with fresh-egg titties and apple asses. Perhaps the thinking behind their employment reaches back to the time when young girls were put in bed with ailing old men in the belief that their vitality would be absorbed by the old dudes through a process of magical sexual osmosis.

"Hungry, Mr. Cant?"

"Starved."

She helped me shift closer to the table, where she placed the tray and wheeled away.

Fried chicken. Good choice, I thought. I felt picnicky, with the scenery and all.

I mulled the questions. The big question, why was I here? Or perhaps, more important, is it over? Is there more to come? Would the evil gods that produced and directed this scenario call for more?

15

The candystriper was back before I finished the meal.

"Dr. Manna will see you now."

Hot expectations surged in my veins at the announcement. I'd get the answers now. Death or deliverance would begin . . . and I was hot for a climax. The candystriper clattered me down the white hallway to His office, deposited me inside, and left without a word.

"Good afternoon, Mr. Cant."

The doctor stood with his back to me, looking through Venetian blind slats held parted with the fingers of his right hand. It struck me as a studied pose. I decided on an attention-getting gambit.

"Your mother sucks lizard eggs. What am I doing here?"

He did not react. He was a cool one and he was letting me know it. He released the parted slats and turned to me with a warm smile that made my own hostility seem uncomfortable and childish. I furrowed my brow and determined that I would not allow myself to be charmed by this man.

"You are here because you were sick. Simply that," he said.

"What is my illness; or as you put it, what *was* my illness?"

"You were mentally ill."

"And now?"

"Now you . . . well, you're getting better."

16

"Good. May I leave? May I go home?" I stood up.

"There are a few loose ends that we should ... or rather *you* should tie together, Mr. Cant."

"Thank you, but I would just as soon do that at home—out of this place, if that's all right with you—which I know it's not." I smiled saccharinely. "Because I am a goddamn captive here; isn't that true, Dr. Banana, or whatever the hell your name is?"

"Where do you work, Mr. Cant?"

"I work at the ... at the ... at ..."

"Do you work?"

"I'm a ... a ..." I struggled to remember.

The bastard's face was inscrutable. Where did I work? What did I do for a living? When I tried to think I had a tip-of-the-tongue feeling that sustained itself painfully, but no answer came.

"You've taken my memory. You drugged me into amnesia."

"Have we, Sebastian? Let's see. Were you in the service?"

"Yes."

"Branch?"

"Air Force."

"Overseas?"

"Viet Nam."

"Action?"

"Some."

"Date of enlistment, Sebastian?"

"May sixteenth, nineteen-sixty-five."

"Discharge?"

"January fourth, nineteen-sixty-eight."

"Serial number?"

"Two-one-nine four-five four-oh-six."

"Well?"

"So I remember the service. What about afterwards? What about a year ago? What about a week before I got in this damn place?"

"Relax, Sebastian. You will see that everything's all right. You will understand, accept, and ultimately go beyond understanding and acceptance. Now, you asked me, what about a week before you came in here, right?"

"Yes."

"Okay, let's see . . . when was the last time you ate roast duck?"

I thought for only a second and it came to me in detail and technicolor. "Thanksgiving."

"With whom?"

"Mary. She invited me . . ."

"To her home for Thanksgiving dinner, right?"

"Yes."

"Now think, Sebastian, where were you when you were brought to the hospital?"

"I was in a bar. The Sands. I was there by myself. The cops nailed me outside . . . I still don't know what for . . . and I was taken to the hospital."

"How long before that . . . before the bar and the arrest . . . did you have Thanksgiving dinner with Mary?"

I couldn't remember.

Satisfied with my puzzlement, he began questioning again as if I were "it" in a game of blindman's buff and he were giving me a few playful extra spins before letting me crash about.

"What high school did you go to?"

"Coolidge."

"Grammar school . . . elementary?"

"Public School Sixteen, Bronx."

"Did you get a gift for graduation from grammar school?"

"Yes, a watch from my father."

"Do you remember what kind, by any chance?"

"Yes, as a matter of fact, I do. It was a Bulova with a gold expansion band."

"Did you go anyplace to celebrate your graduation?"

"Yes. We . . . my parents and I and my brother and sister . . . we went to a restaurant . . . Minolli's . . . we had a spaghetti dinner. It was a kind of a present along with the watch because I got honors in math. I was failing but I studied real hard . . . for my father. He rewarded me with the watch and the dinner." I spilled out the details, grateful that I could remember with such lucidity. Grateful that I still had a memory.

"That is remarkable. Don't you agree, Sebastian, that to remember the details of such a long ago event is remarkable? Can you remember, I wonder, what you were wearing?"

"Blue suit . . . navy blue . . . white-on-white shirt and tie. White-on-white was a craze then. . . ."

"What was the argument about?" He was suddenly leaning forward on the edge of his chair and his eyes were searching mine. The bastard was trying to see into my brain.

"What argument? I don't remember any argument."

"The argument in your office, Sebastian."

"My office? What the hell are you talking about?"

"In your office, at work, two weeks before you entered the hospital."

"How the hell can I remember anything that happened where I work when I can't even remember what the hell I do for a living?"

He stared at me, the lower part of his eyelids raised in study. He wasn't sure if I was telling the truth. He rubbed his chin with his forefinger and thumb, and his gaze grew intense and hypnotic.

"I want you to picture yourself standing outside of Minolli's restaurant the day of your graduation from Public School Sixteen. You have finished eating and you are outside Minolli's. Are you alone?" He was talking as if I were hypnotized. I wasn't, of course, but I wanted to answer. I wanted to play his game so I could get my own answers.

"I'm alone."

"Your parents?"

"Inside."

"Why?"

"I don't know."

"Now, look at the entrance to Minolli's. Someone has come out. Who is it?"

"My . . . my sister." I became uncomfortable.

"What's wrong, Sebastian?"

"She's bleeding. She has blood on her face . . . on her forehead. She has a cut on her forehead and it's bleeding like mad. She's crying. She's angry at me . . . no, she's hurt . . . she's hurt and crying because I hurt her. I cut her face . . ."

"With what? And why?"

"I don't know."

"I will tell you, Sebastian. You argued in the restaurant. Violently. You tore the watch your father gave you from your wrist and threw it in your sister's face with all your strength and then ran from the restaurant. That is what happened."

"Why?"

He totally ignored the question.

21

"Sebastian, do you understand the meaning of the phrase 'associative reaction'?"

"I think so."

"If I said 'red' and you replied 'blood'; or if I said 'orange' and you said 'juice,' those would be associative responses, right? But not *reactions*. Do you remember those old comedy movies where the sound of a horn or bell or a certain word would plunge a peaceful character into a violent rage?"

"What are you trying to tell me, Doctor?"

He leaned forward again, and with an effort to be careful, to reassure, he said, "One doesn't feed a steak to an infant. One feeds food that is easy to digest or the baby may choke, may strangle. You're an intelligent man, Sebastian. You will put the pieces together. You will see the whole of it and not be frightened. If you were to see all of it now, at once, you would just reject it out of hand. You couldn't handle it all at once and accept. Believe me, please."

He stood up and walked to the window and raised the blinds to reveal a red twilight sky.

"Lovely, isn't it?"

"Yes."

"It's a lovely world, Sebastian. There are a few things, a few people . . . sick, confused children, no more, no less . . . that make some things not so pretty. But tonight, from here, it's a pretty world, do you agree?"

"Yes, it's a pretty sunset, anyway."

He understood from my tone that I was not convinced of his benevolence.

"You like John Macky, don't you, Sebastian?"

"John who?"

"John Macky, the orderly in . . . Intensive Care."

"Oh, yeah. He's OK."

Without knowing really why, I did instinctively trust this John-the-orderly.

Dr. Bananas pushed a button on a squawk box on the coffee table. "Have John Macky of D.C. come to my office, please. And ask him to bring a change of clothes for Mr. Cant."

"Yes, Dr. Manna."

Manna, Bananas, I was close. He walked back to the window and clasped his hands behind his back in what I always thought of as a peculiarly English pose. English Leftenant, to be exact, about to announce something of import, and giving the proclamation an appropriate prelude of stern musing. I was about to ask him what D.C. stood for when he turned and spoke.

"You are free to leave Sunnyview, Sebastian. There are no bars, and there are no fences, but you will not leave. You will not because you are intelligent, and intelligence includes within itself the quality, or, depending on your point of view, the weakness of a strong curiosity."

He studied my face and I his for a very long moment. A knock, and the door opened and a red curly head peeked round.

"Come in, John. You know Mr. Cant."

"Yes. How are you doing, Mr. Cant?" John-the-orderly smiled. He did have a good open face, I thought. He handed me a pair of white trousers, white shirt, socks, and sneakers. Bananas invited me to get out of the wheelchair and into the clothes. I complied while he continued.

"John lives on the hospital grounds. Why don't you show Sebastian around our place, John? Can you do that?"

"Yes, sir. I'm off duty in about an hour."

"You are off duty now."

"Thank you, sir."

I finished changing into the white shirt and pants and Bananas put his hand on my left shoulder and leaned back a bit in appraisal. "You look strong enough to get about walking, Sebastian."

"I feel strong enough, Doctor." I didn't like calling him "Doctor." It's a title I always associated with respect and a certain amount of awe and I didn't like Bananas.

He turned my shoulder and steered me to the door. "Relax. Enjoy our clean country air. The stars are simply brilliant up here. I think, Sebastian, that you'll feel better with each new day, and soon better than you've ever felt in your life."

"Where are we exactly, Doctor? Where is Sunnyview located?"

"In the country, Mr. Cant. In the clean, fresh-aired country."

"The one I was born in, I hope."

"Ha! Good. You have a bright sense of humor."

"Too kind. When are we going to have another *chat*? I'd like to learn as much as possible as soon as possible. And one more thing . . . am I going to have any more of those . . . those dreams?"

"I don't think so. Do you?"

I turned, angrily brushing his hand from my shoulder. "How the hell do I know?"

His smile fled. His very gray eyes became very gray cool.

"I think you will realize, Mr. Cant, that you are past a certain stage."

John eyed the floor nervously. There was nothing to be said, no alternative action but to leave. The sun was going down and "God" was closing his office. We left and soon John and I were strolling across my new campus.

Saint John-the-orderly was in a tour guide mood. On your left is the such-and-such, to your right is the so-and-so. Garrulous and animated.

"Slow down, John."

"I'm sorry. I forgot, you haven't been on your feet in a while, have you?"

We had come to a little knoll and a shade tree and I elected to lie down on this particularly inviting patch of grass, silhouetting John between me and the setting sun.

"I really don't want a guided tour, John, as much as I want some anwers."

He tightened, as I expected.

"Sit down, John. I'm not going to put you on the spot." I, of course, was going to.

He crouched, sitting on one heel, and pulled a tuft of grass apart idly. "I can't tell you much. That is, I'm not permitted to."

"Why, John? Will you be shot as a traitor?"

He smiled, "No, hardly. It's better for you, Mr. Cant . . ."

"Sebastian."

"It's better for you, Sebastian, if you learn in stages, like Dr. Manna said."

"Look, Saint John . . ."

"Saint John?"

"It's nothing. I have a thing about names."

"Been called worse."

"Answered?"

"Depends on the caller."

"Enough profundities, Saint John. Let's attack the trivia; like, am I really free to leave this joint? If I were suddenly to cut and run, would you pull out a little steel whistle and set the camp to howling with sirens? Would there be barking dogs and me trying to lose them by

26

trudging up a stream through the forest darkly?"

He sat back on his rump, resting on his palms.

"There's a simple way to find out," and he gestured an extended hand toward the distant bordering wood.

I panned from the Saint's cherubic face across the rolling lawns dotted with walking and seated white uniforms to the edge of the surrounding forest. It was closest in its meandering border about eighty yards due left.

"Goodbye," I said.

"Goodbye," said John.

In a flat second I was pumping arms and legs across the crabgrass. When I reached the trees and shot a look back at the Saint, he and two white-frocked cronies were sardonically waving me goodbye with handkerchiefs. I collapsed to my knees grinning back at them, and for the first time since my arrival at this strange place, I felt not friendless, not paranoid, but reasonably, and at least momentarily, safe.

I walked slowly back toward them, wheezing and sweating from the short-lived but intense exercise. They started toward the dormitory waving at me to follow and I waved back a gesture indicating they should proceed. I was not in the best physical condition and in no mood to hustle to catch up to them. When I finally reached the building, I entered to find John alone at a stereo. I sat in a saucer-shaped chair that was surprisingly comfortable and listened to the music melodiously apropos of the setting, which I can tell you was one of ethereal beauty. White marble, white carpeting, lush and thick. Cut-glass coffee tables holding baskets of fruit and flowers . . . and the girls. The girls, walking, sitting, serving drinks, clad in wispy fairy swirls of pastel pinks and blues and greens. Not one daring to be less than pretty and most, angelically beautiful.

"I have died and gone to heaven."

"Not really."

"Not really, but close."

"Close." John's eyes twinkled over his glass as he sipped his drink. "Would you like a guided tour of our humble home, Mr. Cant?"

"Yes, I would, Mr. Macky."

"Good," he said and finishing his drink, proceeded to do so.

The most noteworthy thing about the decor was the color, or really the lack of it. The walls, ceilings, and even the furniture, were in varying tones of white. The upstairs was simply a long hallway of bedrooms conspicuously lacking doors. A fact on which I commented: "No doors?"

"No doors."

"Why not?"

"Why doors?"

28

"Well, because."

"Gee, Sebastian, you have such a way with words."

"And you, Saint John, such a subtle humor. Are they ... uh ... coed?"

"Dirty old man."

"Did I ask that with a leer?"

"Yes. They're hardly co-educational, but both sexes, yes, and the rooms are assigned as they are needed and become available, sir."

Downstairs consisted of two large day rooms, one called the Winter room and the other the Summer room. At the end of the Winter room was a long dining area with a circular fireplace at either end. The center of the house was a huge open kitchen wherein a black cook, sporting *mammalia gigantea*, marched about preparing food and behaving in a quaintly authoritarian manner.

"Getcha han's outa my soup, John Macky!"

"Our cook," he ignored. "Beloved Aunt Jemima."

Ordered to leave with a regal flourish of her soup ladle, we made for the Summer room with a glass of mango juice and a grab-hand of tasty cookies.

"Don't just sit there doing your twinkling-over-the-glass thing ... 'splain." I said.

" 'Splain? What do you want 'splained?"

"What is all this? Just what the hell is all this? I admit I'm duly impressed and you know it. That's what all your cutesy looks are about, right? You're just coming off, John, like a gay mortician. I want some goddamn answers."

"Ask me."

"And you'll answer all my questions?"

"Take it easy, Sebastian, I'm not trying to be coy or flip."

"I like you, John," I said plaintively, "so I don't want to get angry at you. But I'm frustrated." He understood. "What exactly is this place?" I asked.

"A hospital."

"A mental hospital?"

"Yes."

"Where are we?"

"Geographically?"

I brought up the corners of my mouth and lowered my eyelids to indicate impatience.

"Sorry. I can only tell you, Sebastian, that we are in California."

"Northern? Southern?"

"Sorry."

"Okay. You can't tell me exactly. Not won't, but can't, right?"

He nodded and shrugged his shoulders.

"All right, John. If this is a mental hosp . . ." Suddenly a little blonde in pink was at my elbow. Without a word she took my near-empty glass from my hand and held it up in the gesture that asked if another was desired.

"Yes, thank you," I said.

She took John's from the coffee table and he nodded he would like another. She went away on quiet bare feet. I forgot the train of thought she had interrupted.

"Are they all nurses, John?"

"They all work here."

"Every one's a winner. Were they hired for their looks?"

"No." He smiled.

"But they're all so goodlooking."

"Some were born that way."

I had turned to look about the room, but my eyes came back to John at the implication of his remark.

"*Some* were born that way?"

He shifted, uncomfortably. What was matter-of-fact to him was clearly not to me, and he was relieved at the interruption of the pink lady returning with our refilled glasses. John looked into his glass as he sipped, hoping that I would let the matter drop. I wouldn't.

"If only some were born that way, then others were not; they were *made* that way." I stared at John, John stared at his mango juice.

"Okay, Sebastian, some were, as you put it, made that way." He didn't look up until he had finished the sentence.

"Plastic surgery? Cosmetic surgery?"

"Nothing wrong with a pretty face, is there?"

He clearly did not want to say flat out that

31

he wouldn't tell me certain things. He preferred to indicate obliquely that I was approaching a taboo area and should back off. John Macky was a sensitive man. He found refusal to reveal truth difficult and lying unbearable, but he did want me to know some of the truth. He wanted me to prepare myself like a man who is about to dive into a cold sea, by splashing my body with the cold water of some of *the picture.* I relieved his tension because I liked him.

"You too, John? Cosmetic surgery?"

He broke into a broad grin and we both laughed. It was patently funny to think that any plastic surgeon would *create* his plain corn muffin face and then splatter it with freckles to boot.

"Hi," she said, and there she was. Her dress was of light and dark greens, a white flower in her dark hair, and she was Julie Goldberg, long-legged and delicious.

"Hi, Julie. You know Sebastian. . . . Just get off?"

"Yes." She brushed her hair back from her forehead, sat down, and smiled at me, and I took in a heavy irregular deep breath.

"How are you, Mr. Cant?"

"Fine."

"You look just great. A lot better than when I saw you last."

"Thanks."

"How do you like our little place?"

"Very nice."

"So you're not going to run through the woods and leave us?" She laughed. She flicked a knowing glance at John, paused, sipped, and explained, "I was one of your admirers waving you goodbye."

"I know. That's what stopped me." I didn't know, of course, because I couldn't make out gender much less faces at that distance, but I lied in my lowest, sexiest tones because it was a good opportunity to begin my fatal mating dance.

"I knew you would, Seb. That's why I waved." She was responding nicely to my first ruffling of feathers. John excused himself.

"You're a fine looking woman, Julie," I said, hoping my eyes were brown limpid pools.

"You have a nice personality, Sebastian." She smiled. She had a lot of imp in her. I sat back comfortably and let my eyes roam her face and body. She blatantly let her face show that she enjoyed the attention. Saint John returned, too soon.

"You'll be seeing Dr. Manna again tomorrow."

"Was there a notice in the men's room?"

"Very funny. I knew before, I just thought to tell you now."

"What can *you* tell me, Julie? What can *you* tell me about Sunnyview?"

33

She reached over the table and took my hand.

"Just not to worry. That everything's Okay. That I like you."

Dinner consisted of barbequed spareribs with corn, yams, and string beans that were grown, John explained, on the hospital grounds. There was some joke about Rebecca of Sunnyview Farm not worth repeating. Afterwards, we sat around the fireplace with our feet kicked up on the encircling brickwork and sipped a delicious blackberry wine. Someone started to sing an old song softly and we all joined in. Huge logs crackled and glowed in the fire, and Julie took my left hand and entwined our fingers. We sat like that for more than an hour, then the room began to stir with people getting up and leaving. Julie rose, kissed me on the cheek and said goodnight, and John led me upstairs to my room.

"Corner room. You got lucky." John gestured that I enter.

"Corners are only valuable in real estate, Saint John, and even that's questionable."

"A corner room means windows on two walls, turkey. One more than the other rooms."

He was right, of course, and the view of the moonlit lawns and bright stars was pretty. John leaned against the sill of the doorless doorway while I moseyed about inspecting what was to be my home for . . . how long? It occurred to me with a rush of anxiety that sat me down that I was pleasantly retiring in a room in a hospital still without knowing what the hell I was doing there. Worse, I had allowed myself to be lulled into a state of accepting and aiding in my own incarceration.

"Feeling trapped, Seb?"

"Do you also read fortunes?"

"It's easy to tell and easier to understand."

"So saith John-the-orderly."

"Thou mayest leave, my son." He placed his palm on my head in mock blessing.

"Getteth thy dumb hand off my head."

He flicked on the night-table lamp, opened a bureau drawer, and withdrew some magazines, which he tossed on the bed.

"Readeth and sleepeth."

"No help, Saint John? No encouraging words? I'm scared, Saint John, I'm getting downright nervous." He paused in the doorway before leaving.

"Did anyone stop you this afternoon when you made a run for it?"

"No. But I still want some more answers, and soon."

"You'll see Bananas, as you call him, tomorrow morning after breakfast."

"John?"

"Yeah?"

"You're asking me to relax and settle down to sleep in a room in a strange place called

Sunnyview without telling me why I'm here or for how long."

"Sebastian, do you trust me?"

"I don't know why, Saint John, but, yeah, I trust you."

"I'll see you in the morning."

I heard him moving down the hallway, and the sounds of hushed conversations from other bedrooms. A brand new pair of flannel pajamas was draped over the end of the bed. I undressed and put it on, slipped between cool, fresh sheets, and switched off the lamp. Bananas was right, I thought. The stars are brilliant up here . . . wherever up here is. I looked at the sky through the uncurtained window for a long time, and as my eyelids grew heavy it occurred to me that I was entering an undrugged sleep for the first time in recent memory.

4.

I heard something and turned onto my back and looked to the doorway. I saw only the pink of a nightgown and the white of her smile.

"Can I sleep with you?"

I didn't answer. I simply didn't believe the dream. She came out of the faint back-lighting of the hallway, into the shadowed room. Close to the bed. Now lifting a corner of sheet and blanket, her voice so soft and breathy, she asked again.

"Can I sleep with you?"

The wine-hot corpuscles were surging so strongly all witticisms fled in the face of a swallowed "Yes." She came into my bed, knees up, covers over, legs straightening and shifting and finding her comfortable hold on me as if we had slept together a hundred times. Familiar and relaxed and hot. "Goddamn," I breathed. "You're a lot of woman, Julie."

I was a rock in a minute. Her eyes and smile luminescent in the dimness, she let go a sigh as she took me inside with her soft hand and pulled my head to her mouth. Afterward, she laid her hot cheek on my chest and told me she loved me. Honestly and with feeling. She meant it.

The next morning I awoke to the sound of my own silly-ass sighs and moans. The room was filling with bright sunlight that illuminated the microscopic dust particles in the air. I lazily puffed a chunk of air through them, watching the puff of air defined by the dust particles move as surely as if I had given it power of its own. I was alone. I wondered aloud, "What time is it?" On cue, a head peeked in, said "Breakfast," and was gone again. So many thoughts and questions flooded my brain that I could not concentrate on any one, so I blinked my mind and washed them away, leaving only the reminiscence of the previous night and the niceness of the morning.

I broke bread, or kaiser rolls to be exact, with Saint John, who explained that Julie had to eat and run but had deposited with him a wish that I have a pleasant morning and a request that I join her for lunch.

"When?"

"She said she would be here at twelve and to wait if she was late."

"That's all?"

"Like I say, she said to wish you a pleasant morning."

"You know, John, I slept with that girl last night."

John grinned in a saintly way.

"Don't just sit there . . . you have egg on your chin . . . don't just sit there, say something."

He wet his napkin with his tongue and wiped his chin.

"Is it gone?"

"Yeah, damn it, it's gone. Well?"

He folded his napkin twice and dropped it on the table.

"What do you want me to say, Sebastian? Do you want me to ask you how it was? Do you want me to ask the details? Or do you want my blessings, my son?"

There was no getting angry at the saint. Not for me, anyway. Besides, what *did* I want him to say?

"When do I see Bananas?"

"Dr. Manna," he corrected. He stood up. "Now."

"Now?"

"He waits." I was suddenly nervous. John was standing over me, leaning over me, it seemed.

"Okay, okay, don't rush me." I sipped at the untasty dregs of cooled coffee, stalling.

"I'm not rushing you," he said.

Finally, with a "Let's go," I stood up and we left the dining room. I really didn't want to see Bananas. The fact of the matter was, he scared the shit out of me.

Walking across the parklike grounds in my fresh white clothes, I felt oddly cliché. Like the lead in a "B" movie about an astronaut captured by friendly Martians. I half expected a mad director to leap from behind the bougainvillaea yelling, "Cut! Cut! Print it!"

But I trusted Saint John and I didn't feel threatened. I was not walled in or shackled, and any time I wanted to I could break and run and no one would stop me. That proven fact alone kept back the panic.

I sat outside of Bananas's office for a long time, waiting as the saint instructed. I sat there in my white uniform, in the white hallway on a white bench, idly speculating on the color of my feces if I had an irrepressible bowel movement. I decided the decor demanded either Desert Sand or Eggshell. His door was closed and there was no sound from his office and I wondered if he would arrive soon or whether he were already there engaging in what used to be called self-abuse. I strained to listen and thought I heard panting.

The door clicked open, ending the satisfying imaginings, and there he stood, businesslike and ingratiatingly warm and polite.

40

"Good morning, Mr. Cant. Won't you come in, please."

I hadn't noticed it before, but the office was in stark contrast to the colorless hallway. But I was, of course, now beginning to notice more and more. My perception was increasing as my mind was clearing.

There were several paintings, good ones, on the wood-paneled walls. There were vases of fresh flowers, live plants, and *objets d'art* on small decorative tables. There was a large bank of books, medical texts mostly, and a wet bar.

"Sit down, Mr. Cant." He gestured to one of two big black Naugahyde chairs guarding the coffee table. I did. He did not. Rather, he walked to the bar and asked if I wanted a drink.

"This early?"

"Are you one of those nothing-before-five-o'clock and then gin-until-unconscious types?"

"No, but no thanks."

"A little wine," he insisted. "Please join me, Mr. Cant. Jefferson, you know, said we ought to be sure to produce good wines lest we turn to hard liquor. I'm paraphrasing, of course, but the thought is 'sensible.' "

"Okay," I said. "A little wine never hurt anyone."

"Good, good." He was pleased as only the anti-teetotaler can be pleased at finding a fellow. He handed me a glass with a smile and turned and walked to the window. I had the feeling that this was all done before, many, many, times: the gesture, the timing, all of it tried and tested to perfect the recipe that would never fail. Smooth and finished and polished to the needle point. I was the plebe about to be initiated and Bananas had danced this waltz a hundred times before with other plebes at other times.

"A toast?" He raised his glass above his arched eyebrows with a half turn toward me. The ham. Even the lighting was right, his face etched perfectly, and the wine illuminated by the morning sun.

"A toast," I okayed.

"To ..." and he reached his glass out toward me ... "to Sunnyview."

There was challenge in the gesture akin to the loyalty challenge intrinsic in the Nazi salute, and I was tempted to reply, "Heil, Sunnyview," but I did not. I said simply, "To Sunnyview," and drained my glass.

"Thirsty?"

"Nervous."

"There's no need, Sebastian. No need at all. More wine?"

"Yes, thank you."

He hustled over to restore my empty glass and take it to the bar for a refill. He was glad I was drinking. He wanted me bombed, I was sure.

"You're your own pre-operative anesthesiologist, aren't you, Doctor?"

He handed me my second drink.

"You're very perceptive, Sebastian. Yes, I do want you to be relaxed."

"I'm perceptive? You're the sharp one among all us two people. You're a real fox, Doctor." I raised the wine to my lips and mumbled "The Banana Fox" into my glass and chuckled at the baptism. He heard me.

"The Banana Fox? Oh, yes of course, you refer to me as Dr. Bananas. The Banana Fox, eh? Not bad."

"I don't like that business," I said angrily.

"What business?"

"You know exactly what I mean. Knowing what I say privately. Do you have my room bugged? Is John wired for sound?"

"John is not wired. Your room is, yes."

His plainly honest answer disarmed me. He caught the moment, placed his glass on the table, and sat down opposite me. He spoke quickly but evenly.

"What is Sunnyview?"

"A hospital," I answered.

It was patently a hospital and of course that was, therefore, not the answer. Not the answer *we* wanted.

"It's a mental hospital." Strike two. I knew it and he knew it. He peered into my eyes.

Deep into me. There was something in the drink. He had drugged me.

"What is Sunnyview?" he asked again.

"It's a place that people are taken to . . ." and as I verbalized the whole of it, I began to urinate in the chair. "It's a place where people are brainwashed . . ." my thighs were soaking and I was feeling faint. "Where people learn the . . ."

"The Truth, Sebastian."

I felt very cold and I began to shake and yet my blood was hot. My face was hot.

"No!" I screamed, and scared the hell out of myself. He spoke quickly and evenly to shorten the unendurable pain. To pull the tooth's bloody mass in a yank. To chop the live, putrid limb in a single merciful slash.

"Your name is Sebastian Cant and you killed your daughter by pushing her from a window five stories high. You killed your own daughter, your flesh and blood. You pushed her out the window and killed her."

"I didn't! I didn't! I have no daughter!" But as I yelled this at him, the truth was on me. I *had* a daughter. Annie. The nightmarish scenario flashed before my mind's eye. I saw little Ann's face, her blonde hair and blue dress ruffled in the wind, and the flapping window curtains, and I passed out.

"Come on, Mr. Cant. Come on, Mr. Cant.

Come on, Mr. Cant. Come on, Mr. Cant." They were singing. The beasts, the witches. They looked horrible in the light of the reading lamp but I knew what they wanted, the beasts, the witches. I bore down and finally the plastic bottle began to fill.

"He's filling it, he's filling it. That's good, Sebastian, that's very good."

They danced around the light, their monster shadows leaping about the walls. They took the bottle and poured the urine into three fine Waterford crystal goblets, toasted me, rolled their eyes, and drank it down. The beasts. The witches. I knew they were Waterford glasses. I could tell. Fine beautiful crystal in their evil clawing hands. The beasts.

5.

JULIE stood in the doorway of my room.
"Can I come in?"

I didn't answer. I felt myself starting to cry
and I didn't try to repress the tears and sob-
bing. With a swish of nightgown and bedsheets
she was beside me, holding me to her breasts
and I was crying softly. The free tears and
soft sobs of defeat. I was beaten. Whipped.
This hospital had me scared shitless and the
only thing good or safe in the universe was
Julie. I surrendered to her arms.

The next morning Julie and I showered together in the bath adjoining my room. It was a
sexless ritual even though she soaped me down
with a lathered washcloth and patted me dry
with towels afterwards.

"Feel better?"

I didn't answer her and through breakfast I spoke to no one. Not out of determined refusal, but simply because I was overwhelmed by futility. I was drained of the energy to utter a word of any kind. I moved through the morning inactivities until I was walked to the hospital, guided to Bananas's room, and seated to await the devil.

He came from nowhere and sat across from me. We stared at each other for a measured minute. He breached the silence.

"You still want to know? You still want to know the answers, Sebastian?"

"No, you son-of-a-bitch," I said very calmly. "I don't want to know, I don't care to know. I choose to remain ignorant, thank you just the same."

"Sebastian, your curiosity . . ."

"Bullshit, I don't want to know." He squirmed and smiled only with his teeth.

"I see," he said, and turned to the window.

"What's the matter, Doctor? You seem to be at a loss. You mustn't *bring me around* by coercion. Isn't that it? Have I got it, Doc? Aren't those the rules? But you have used force, haven't you? If feeding me drugs that set me hallucinating to the extent of scaring me shitless isn't force, I don't know what is, you hypocritical bastard."

He spun round on that and set his teeth hard. "It is not force, Sebastian Cant, it is not

47

force! You have seen only nightmares that were buried in your own mind disinterred. It is a cleansing process, and a cauterizing. It is for your good!" He sat down slowly, carefully, ever aware of the value of continuity.

"I don't want to capture your mind, Sebastian, I want to free it. Why do you think I gave you that book of Orwell's? To show you the *other* side."

"*1984?*"

"Yes! *That*, Mr. Cant, is a negative Utopia but that is not what we are about. We don't want to enslave mankind. We want to *free* it. Free it from self-destructive violence. We have the power to do that. Here. Now. If we can do so, what is wrong with that? To put an end to wars, to murder, to assault? And hatred? Is that wrong? Is that an evil goal? A wrong purpose? Look at me, Sebastian. Twelve years ago a man in Akron, Ohio, lured two young girls . . . two children . . . into his car. He drove them to a vacant house on the outskirts of town where he tortured and raped them both. He was caught because a neighbor saw smoke coming from the chimney and thought the police should know that the vacant house was being used." Bananas interrupted himself. "I want to show you something," he said, and he quickly crossed the room and fished a small packet from his desk. He was back in the chair before the dent in the black plastic left by his

officious arse had unformed. He handed me the
packet, which turned out to be a dozen or so
small photographs in booklet form. The cover
simply said "Charles L." and the pictures
showed a man, a woman, and a young girl enjoying a backyard barbeque. Two things were
obvious. Firstly, judging by the camera angle
and the fact that all the shots were apparently
candid, the subjects were unaware they were
being photographed. It looked to be individual
frames of a film shot from a second- or third-
story window. Secondly, from the interplay of
the man, woman, and child (a young girl), this
was a family. A family at home . . . and seem-
ingly loving and happy.

I looked up at Bananas. "Is this the man
you're telling me about?"

"When the police entered the vacant house,
Sebastian, the stench nearly knocked them out.
You see, the smoke the neighbor had seen was
coming from the burning flesh of one of the
girls. He had thrown her lifeless body into the
fireplace and soaked her with gasoline. The
second girl was tied to a chair facing
the hearth. She was alive but catatonic when
the police broke in."

I glanced down at the booklet I held limply
in my lap and flipped through the pictures. One
showed the father hugging his daughter.

"Mind you, he wasn't trying to destroy the
evidence, Sebastian. When the police ques-

tioned him he explained that he was, quote, 'boiling out the sin bubbles.' "

I was staring at the smiling, gentle looking man in the photograph and trying to attach the story to that face.

"Incredible? Incredible that such a propensity for evil could be in the mind of any man? That a man could be so insane? That is not incredible, Sebastian, but I will tell you what *is* incredible. Those photographs, my dear Sebastian, were taken *after* he committed the crime."

My eyes shot up from the booklet.

"Eleven years and two months after, to be exact. The pictures, as you might have guessed, are from a strip of film shot from a distance. They were taken last year and they show Charles L., the doting, loving husband and father, who raped and tortured two girls twelve years ago. That pleasant smiling man killed a child and then set fire to the body to boil out what he called the sin bubbles."

"But how . . . ?"

"How what, Sebastian? How did he get loose? Why isn't he hiding? Why does he seem so normal? Which question shall I answer first? None!" He spat the word out and suddenly stood up and I knew the interview was over. He walked to the back of his desk and pressed a button noiselessly.

"No answers today, Sebastian, save this one

... we did it, Sebastian ... myself and my associates. *We did it.*"

The door opened behind me and a nurse was at my elbow. The bravado I felt moments ago was gone. He took a consoling tack, and put his arm on my shoulder as I walked toward the door.

"Will you come to see me tomorrow morning?"

I nodded.

"Good. About ten o'clock, then. Have a pleasant day. Relax."

Sure I would.

A nurse came in and accompanied me dumbly through the door and down the hall. Then it struck me. So violent was the thought that I felt the taste of vomit. *It was me.* The man in the photograph was *me!* The nurse firmed her support as she felt me weaken.

"Are you all right, Mr. Cant?" Her face was fretful, no doubt reflecting how ill I suddenly looked.

"I'm Okay. I'm Okay. I'm all right," I lied.

"I think we should sit down for a minute. We don't look so well."

"No, I'm Okay. I just need some air."

What I needed was to talk to John Macky. Once outside, some blood must have returned to my face because I was able to persuade Mama to turn me loose.

"I'm Okay," I said again. And again, and

again, until she finally let go of my elbow and I headed beeline to the dormitory and the saint. I found him in the Summer room sipping a drink. I sat down and poured out the interview with Bananas.

". . . then, John, it dawned on me that I was the guy in the photographs. Don't you see, it was *me*. I'm the guy that he said raped those kids that he was talking about. They got me. They used plastic surgery on me . . . simple enough . . . transferred me here . . . simple enough . . . gave me enough drugs to forget. These things can be done . . . hell, I don't have to tell you. You know that's what this place does. Plastic surgery is simple enough . . . then drugs . . . good God. Mother of God. I did *that*. It was me. It was *me*, John."

"This is the part where I slap you."

"What?" I became aware I had the sleeve of Saint John's jacket twisted in my fist. People at nearby tables were staring at us.

"Sorry." I let go and the sleeve of his jacket stayed crumpled where I had held it. With a tug at his cuff to pull out the wrinkles, he sat up and motioned a girl over.

"Have a drink, Sebastian," he said.

"No thanks. Well, yes. Okay. Bring me a straight shot of Bourbon and a tall glass of water." John waved her off to her mission and turned to me.

"You are Sebastian Cant. You are not Charles L."

"Do you know him?"

"I know *of* him. I know of the case. Everyone does." He noted my look and amended: "Everyone at Sunnyview." I looked him over with a reappraising eye. I was becoming aware of just how much more he knew than I. How much, much more he knew, and how little . . . how very little . . . I knew about Sunnyview.

"Do you see Dr. Manna again tomorrow?" he asked.

I nodded.

"Ask him flat out, Sebastian; he'll tell you. You're not Charles L."

The girl arrived with my drink. She was redheaded and, like the others, beautiful. Greeneyed and milk-skinned, with enormous freckled breasts that strained her bodice. I could easily imagine her milking a cow or churning butter. She was wearing a kelly green peasant dress.

". . . there'd be nothing to worry about."

"What? I'm sorry, John."

The girl smiled and left.

"I said, Sebastian, that even if you were Charles L. there'd be nothing to worry about." The saint saw the apprehension rising in my eyes. "But you are not," he added quickly and firmly. "Tomorrow Manna will tell you. Tonight, take my word for it. Why should I lie?"

Why should he? I reasoned, and relaxed a bit.

"How about some golf, Sebastian?" He stood up with the invitation.

"Miniature?"

"Hell no, man, we got nine whole holes. Did I say that?"

"You did."

"Well?"

"Saint John, you're a marvel. I would just love to crack some golf balls."

"Crack, eh? My, we are hostile."

"Well, that's why I'm here, isn't it?" I said this in a light, joking manner, as I rose from my chair, but as the words left my mouth they slowed like the words on a recording slow when the RPM winds down. Everything slowed. And in slow motion the glass slipped from my hands breaking apart melodically when it hit the table, and I was going over backwards clutching the air, and incredibly I was still ending the sentence with the words coming in deep basso slowness. John reached out and my elbow cracked the table on the long way down. God ... damn ... that ... hurt.

"Goddamn, that hurt."

"You *said* that," said John. He and the girl in kelly green and some others had sat me up on the chair and I was rubbing a lump on the back of my noggin. Kelly Green produced a little brown translucent capsule and offered it,

54

advising me to place it in my mouth and bite it.
I took it in my hand and looked at the saint.
He nodded. "It will kill the pain, that's all." I
put it in my mouth and crushed it between my
back molars and the pain in my head was gone.
Instantly. Not eased. Gone.

"Amazing."

"Effective little devils, aren't they?"

He was right, to say the least.

"Damn right. What are they?"

"A concentrated anesthetic that is absorbed
into the bloodstream through the mouth. Very
effective. Very fast. Kills all pains of any intensity from a toothache to a crushed limb instantly, and lasts for at least two hours. I
should have gotten you your kit, but it slipped
my mind."

"Kit? What kit, John?"

In answer he parted his jacket and revealed
a small rectangular leather pouch attached to
his belt. It had no markings and I could see no
flap or opening.

"What is it, a first-aid kit?"

"Sort of."

The people who had gathered had just as
quickly faded, including Kelly Green and her
gigantic boobs.

"What do you suppose made me do my
falling down trick, John?"

"You're just still weak from so much bedtime, Sebastian, and that straight shot of Bourbon was a bit too much."

"Maybe." I doubted it. The bastards were still getting drugs into me. Into my food. I knew it. The bastards.

"Do you still feel like a little golf?"

"I don't know, John, do you think I should?"

"Sure. Do you good. Get some sun. We'll pick up a kit for you on the way to the clubhouse."

As we walked to the glass doors, I glanced back to the table. Kelly Green had picked up the saint's emptied glass and was wiping the table ritualistically. She saw me and smiled. Those breasts would never droop, I mused. Never. I felt the air brush my neck when Saint John opened the doors and she threw me a wink at the moment John tugged my sleeve.

"Goodlooking girl," I said, marching through.

"Yup."

"They're all goodlooking, Saint."

"Yup."

Stop frames of Julie flashed in my mind and I thought of her and the fact I hadn't seen her all day.

"Hi!" John greeted two nurses and an orderly as we passed. The path we walked was distinguished from the rest of the grounds only because the grass was slightly worn down, allowing the beige sandy soil to show through. There were no roads in sight, just thin brownish paths winding over the plain landscape dotted with the inevitable whiteclad walking dolls. One of the nurses we had just passed had dark hair and long legs. I fell into daydreaming about Julie.

"Wake up, Sebastian."

"What?"

"Since you haven't heard a word I said, I assume you were asleep."

"Sorry, John. You're half right, I was dreaming."

We had come to a ranch-type building, rectangular, about twenty feet deep and fifty wide. It, too, was splotchy green and brown. Ugly.

"Someone forgot to paint this building, Saint John."

He smiled.

John headed straight for the only door and held it open for me. The interior looked immediately familiar. There were floor to ceiling compartmentalized olive green metal racks in evenly spaced rows with walking room between, much like a library. There were cards in eye-level slots at the head of each row, no doubt stating the inventory of each row and location of material within each row. Very familiar. Straight inside the doorway was an elbow-high Formica counter on which sat a little inverted dome bell, the kind you slap for service. John slapped the bell. Nothing. A moment's wait and John slapped again. We heard the sound of a toilet flushing, which segued into a door opening, then some shuffling about . . . mild expletives, as something was knocked over and then re-straightened. Finally a portly-type older man emerged from the darkened aisleway. He had a rolled magazine in one hand and a pipe in the other. He stuffed the magazine under the counter and began slapping the pipe against the heel of his hand, emptying nonexistent ashes into a nonexistent ashtray.

"What can I do for you today, John?"

"How are you doing today, Pop?"

(Base supply. That's what it was. This was a supply room exactly like the one in the service at . . . at where? What base? My mind could see the supply room with the crusty supply sergeant just like this old man, and the olive green racks . . . but where? I couldn't remember.)

"This is Sebastian, Pop. Only been here a few days. He could use a kit."

The old man fixed his rheumy eyes on me a moment while he placed the stem of the pipe in his mouth and blew a particularly obstinate bit of nonexistent tobacco out of the air passage. He removed the the pipe with one hand and extended the other to me.

"Sebastian. Never met anyone named Sebastian." His grip was firm and warm.

"To tell the truth, neither have I . . ." I hesitated at what to call him.

"Pop is fine," he allowed.

"Pop," I nodded.

He stuck the pipe back in his mouth and said around it, "One aid kit coming up," and turned and headed for the rear. All he needed was a yachting cap and a limp for perfect characterization.

"Oh, and a map, Pop," the saint called after him.

"Coming up!"

"What's with the pipe, Saint John?"

"You've probably noticed, Sebastian . . ."

"Why don't you call me Seb? Sebastian is cumbersome."

"Okay, Seb. You've probably noticed that nobody around here smokes. But Pop likes his pipe. It's kind of a pacifier for him. A prop . . . you know . . . but he doesn't smoke. No one does."

"Around here," I added.

"Around here," said John, and Pop reappeared.

"One map," and he snapped down on the Formica a wallet-sized laminated card. His other hand held the kit. He turned it over.

"Belt through here," he gestured with a fat forefinger. Resting his elbows on the counter, he aimed the end of the leather box at me and indicated a red curved metallic flap.

"Here's your safety flap."

He flicked it up and exposed a toggle switch underneath like the covered switches on an aircraft cockpit panel.

"Here's your buzz." Pop put the tip of his finger on the exposed toggle.

"Buzz?"

Pop's eyebrows lifted at this one-word question and I wondered why he expected me to know what a buzz switch was. Perhaps, I speculated, the old supply sergeant is a bit senile.

"I'll explain it to him," John said.

Pop's practiced deft forefinger snapped closed the toggle switch cover and flicked open the top of the kit. The hinged top opened to reveal three compartments that didn't go the depth of the box. Obviously the part below the compartments held a mechanism connected with a buzz. Whatever the hell a buzz was. Pop pointed to each of the compartments, explaining:

"Your T's, your P's and Logrin." He was looking and talking at me but he was really telling Saint John. He pointed to, respectively: T's, pink capsules . . . about a dozen; P's, which looked like and probably were more of the same brown translucent capsules I had taken from Kelly Green earlier when I bumped my head in my fall . . . about a dozen of those;

60

and about two dozen brown speckled tablets that Pop called Logrin.

He snapped shut the top and asked John, "Shall I load it?"

John nodded. Pop then turned the box over, caught his nail under the tip of a slim flat bar attached to the bottom of the kit and, lifting it slightly, got his finger underneath and pulled up one end. It was hinged to the bottom of the kit and pulled up with effort to a forty-five-degree angle. From its ratchet sound it was spring-loaded. Pop then put the heels of his hands on the top of the kit and the opposing open bar and, with some effort, forced the bar back into its depression in the bottom of the kit. It clicked shut and was obviously "loaded." He handed me my kit.

"Thank you."

I walked out as John tossed a salute to Pop and held the door for me. I was turning the little leather box over in my hands, poking open the safety cover on the "buzz" and alternately flicking open and snapping shut the top cover.

"Like your toy?"

"These are called P's for Pain, right?" As I asked, I opened the top and poked a finger at the brown translucent capsules. John nodded. Then, poking my finger in the adjacent compartment: "T's?"

"Right."

"For tranquilizers?"

"Correct."

I moved to the speckled tablets. "Logan?"

"Logrin," John corrected. "A sort of . . . well . . . kind of vitamin concentrate combined with . . ."

"Tranquilizer?"

"No, it's hard to explain, Seb. Take one. They're harmless and good for you."

I looked for one of the water fountains I had noticed posted about the grounds and found none near.

"Just chew one, Seb, they're sweet." I popped a tablet in my mouth. Why worry? I thought, they were getting those other type drugs to me in my food anyway, the bastards. I chewed. Tasty.

"Nothing," I commented to John.

"You won't feel anything, that is, not suddenly."

"Will I be able to levitate or will it just knock a few strokes off my game?"

"You'll see."

The building one-hundred yards ahead had a large speckled letter "G" on two sides. G for Golf? Perhaps God or Gorillas. I was prepared for anything. By the time we arrived at the clubhouse, the Logrin had taken effect. The feeling was not a marijuana high and certainly not a drunk by any means. It was a pleasant glow, somewhat like marijuana but without the disjointedness in time continuity.

John smiled just as we reached the clubhouse and asked, "How do you like it?"

"The Logrin?"

"Yes."

"Can it be smoked?"

We entered the clubhouse and its din of golf banter bouncing loudly off the ceiling and walls. The coming and going locker-room chatter and accompanying noisy portage of equipment seemed to be familiar so I presumed that the game was not so new to me.

"Never played?" asked John.

"I don't know," I said and bitterness was on me with the realization that I wasn't even able to remember whether I played golf or not. The bastards. John gently took the club from my hand and said quickly to me, "It's not really important, is it, Seb?" He placed the club in a golf bag and handed the bag to me by the shoulder strap. He had checked out the bags while I was puttering with a putter. Now he slung his bag over his shoulder and invited me to do the same. I did and we trudged down the path to the first tee to begin probably the silliest game ever invented by *Homo erectus*.

I was on the first green in two shots, surprising both myself and the saint, who obviously by his skill, had played often. I had strung the kit on my belt in the clubhouse and at the third tee, before I stepped up for my shot, I asked John what the "buzz" was for.

"To call for help," I suggested, "like if you have a heart attack or something?"

"Something like that."

"Now what kind of an answer is that, John? I mean, I got the thing strapped on, I ought to know what it's for."

He sat on the edge of one of those little wooden loveseat benches, placed at each tee so golfers can rest periodically from their sport of strength-draining violence. He held his club at the shaft near the head, with the thumbs and forefingers of both hands, alternately letting it drop and raising it again while sighting the ground along the shaft like a bombardier. Probably tracking a creeping-creature target in the grass. I was irritated at his indifference.

"Well, John?"

He got up and cleaned the face of his club with the rag hanging at the ball washing hydrant.

"It gets you help, Seb, that's what—nothing more. Why are you irritated, and, if I may say so, paranoid still?"

"John, shall I tell you my favorite Paranoid joke? This guy," I raved, not waiting for an answer, "goes to a psychiatrist. He tells the shrink that men are following him with knives and mean to kill him. 'Well,' says the shrink, 'you obviously are suffering from paranoia. With some treatments you will be cured.' So the guy goes to the shrink every day for weeks and continues to tell of his delusions about assassins, and the doctor continues to assure him he will get well. Well, one day the guy stumbles into the shrink's office and falls on his face with a kitchen knife protruding from his back. Up jumps the doctor. 'Congratulations,' he says, 'you are not paranoid!'"

John laughed. "That's pretty good. I hadn't heard that one."

"Well, damn it," I said, hotly. "I have been drugged into hallucinating . . . and you know it; and lied to . . . and you know it. So don't give me any hogwash that my fears are imagined. They are real."

"You've made your point, Seb." He took practice swings between sentences. "The buzz will bring aid. (Swing.) The aid will be medical. (Swing.) The aid will also be protective." (Swing.)

"Protective?"

"Yes." He stopped and rested the heels of his hands on the club. "We have a security force here." I nodded and gave him a cynical, thin-lipped grimace. "Well, we're not perfect here, Seb. We have occasional thievery . . . assault sometimes. Then, of course, since we are not fenced in, an occasional hunter stumbles into Sunnyview, or campers, or even a plain old-fashioned hobo."

"And whoever spots the intruder," I said, "presses his buzz."

"Yes."

"And what do you do with him, John, when your SS troops collar him? Do they hypodermic air bubbles into his bloodstream and bury him in the south forty?" Yells from the last hole indicated a desire to play through if we weren't going to get hustling.

"Hardly," was the saint's reply to my speculated fate of the hypothetical hobo.

I cracked a ball hard off the tee, high and up the middle. The foursome coming from the green behind us yelled their thanks, and we trudged up the fairway.

"What do you do, Saint? Or maybe I should say, what *have* you done with people who stumble across your Shangri-la?"

"We don't kill them."

"That's half an answer, the negative half."

John stopped walking and assumed a stance over his ball. He took a few practice swings and I marveled that he had the concentration to be looking for his ball as we walked and talked. My mind was not on the game but rather on the accompanying conversation. John stepped closer to the ball and chipped it on the green. It was a nice shot. He was pretty good. He slipped the iron into his bag, which was lying on the grass, hefted it, and slung it over his shoulder.

"Where's your ball?" he asked.

"Screw it! What do you do with them . . . what do you do with intruders, John!"

"We turn them around and send them home."

"Just like that."

"Not quite."

"Then what? Tell me, John, I want to know. Do you absorb them? Do you indoctrinate them into the Sunnyview 'Club'? Is that it?"

"Sometimes." He stopped walking, unhooked his thumb from the bag's shoulder strap and gestured emphatically with both hands. "Look, what do you want from me, Seb? You know we're isolated here and we don't crave publicity, to put it mildly. You must also know by now, or at least I hope you know, that we're not malevolent. We don't harm our own, nor do we harm strangers, but we do have occasional uninvited guests. We also have scientific solutions to solve such problems and they certainly don't consist of killing people and burying them in the south forty, as you so colorfully put it. We are very scientifically advanced, Seb. Certainly beyond such unoriginal and crude solutions. Look, put your hand on the ground." He demonstrated and I reluctantly imitated, squatting and pressing my palm on the grassy turf. "It's warm." It was. Warm as the hood of a car over a heated engine.

"Steam pipes?"

"Uh-uh. Nothing so archaic. The soil is impregnated with fine metallic grains composed of an alloy that permits conduction of electricity, like the element of a toaster but without . . ."

The foursome to the rear had resumed their banshee invitations, nipping John in midthought. He gave up.

"Pick up your canvas albatross, Seb, and let's cash in. The game is getting in the way of conversation and those four in back may wet their pants if they can't play through."

"Excellent suggestion." I picked up my bag and headed for the clubhouse, allowing my lost ball immortality.

We conversed not at all on the hike back to the clubhouse. Halfway, I shifted my golf bag from right to left shoulder to distribute the chafing. I was sweaty and tired.

"Strap cutting you?" John asked.

"A little. Out of shape."

"Not surprising, Seb. You've been out of bed less than a week. Take a P pill for that shoulder and a Logrin behind it."

"I can handle it."

"We find nothing," he said dryly, "praiseworthy or heroic in the pointless endurance of any pain."

I thought to say to John that pain seemed to me to be part of being human, just as death was part of life, but I said nothing. I acquiesced to his logic instead, popping open the kit with my free hand, and fishing out a little brown capsule which I swallowed easily. No shoulder pain. Then a Logrin to munch on, and when I did John said, "Now that's a lot better, isn't it?" and I thought in reply, "It sure is." It was really a very pleasant day.

"Heineken," I ordered, and John added his request for a Scotch and water, and the pretty dark-haired waitress in black tights smiled a "Yes, sir." This *nineteenth hole* was quite nice. It was a perfect circle with a circular bar at the hub and every table had an unobstructed view. From our position, the golf course fence ran under us and straight out about a hundred yards, then banked left ninety degrees to enclose the course behind us and to our left. At the upper right lay the main building, three stories, of ugly brown and green. Between it and us was the dormitory and a few minor buildings all with large letters on their sides. Identifiable with a guide, I thought, and I reached to my hip pocket for the small map Pop had given me, which I had placed in my wallet. As I was hunched up reaching, the waitress arrived with our drinks and the reaching for my wallet made me notice what I had overlooked till then . . . no money changed hands at Sunnyview, and I wondered how many other obvious things about this strange little society had escaped my conscious awareness.

The waitress, dark-haired and pretty,

prompted thoughts of Julie, and I wondered when I would see her again. She poured John his whiskey and me my beer. The foamy cold brew looked quenchingly good but the Logrin made me so comfortable as to take the edge off. I decided then that uncomfortable sweat and fatigue are necessary to the full enjoyment of cold beer.

"Beer, John, is a drink far removed from candlelight. It had to have been invented under the broiling sun, concocted by a toiling farmer or a salt-burnt fisherman. There is wine in heaven, no doubt, but beer is, by its nature, part of the grime and sweat of earth. I once read a news story about a little old man who survived the sinking of his fishing boat by tearing loose the small wooden bait tank and crawling inside. He bobbed around in the ocean swells for all of fifty-odd hours without a drop of drinkable water, until he was sighted by a Navy destroyer and hauled aboard. The first thing this browned, emaciated old fisherman asked for was a cold beer and a cigarette. Not water. Not steak and potatoes, but a beer and a cigarette! But could you imagine him asking for wine? Never. And those Navy men, bless their salty hearts, brought him his cold beer and lit him a cigarette. He took a couple of deep drags on the cigarette . . . the report went on . . . he quaffed a couple of healthy swallows of beer, and poured the rest of it over his grinning upturned face. That's beer at its ultimate. That is what the beloved brew was born to.

"Whiskey, on the other hand, was not invented, Saint John, it was discovered. It is, as all you Irishmen know, a recipe conceived in purgatory by a malevolent crone, best consigned to use on festering wounds or at festive wakes."

"Are you going to drink your beer or write a poem about it?"

John's remark pulled me out of the day-dreamy level and I took a quick swallow to help bring reality in focus. I looked hard at him.

"Tell me straight, John, if not disposal in the south forty, what *do* you do with the occasional stranger who drops into your sterile Garden of Eden?"

The saint took a sip of his drink, placed his glass on the table, and began rotating it absent-mindedly. "You said . . . or rather you asked . . . if we absorbed them."

"Yes. Do you?"

"Sometimes we do, Seb, but only if all factors prescribe that alternative; the main one," he wagged a finger, "being a voluntary, *voluntary*," he repeated for emphasis, "desire to stay."

I took a swallow of beer. "And if there is no desire to stay?"

71

"Then we send him back where he came from."

"Oh, come on, Saint. What are you saying? That you take him back out in the forest primeval blindfolded and make him promise to count to one hundred while you beat it?"

"Of course not."

"Well?"

"Look, Seb, a lot of this . . . well, a lot of what you're questioning you're going to find out about soon. Starting tomorrow, I think. But you should get it all the proper way and from the proper person."

"Bananas?"

He smiled and acceded again to my dubbing. "Yes, Bananas."

"Look, John, you can understand my anxiety, can't you? I mean, if it weren't for my curiosity over what the hell this place is all about, I'd be long gone. Over the hill." I made an accompanying arcing gesture with my hand.

"Would you?"

"Well, maybe not." (I had a strong feeling of having said the wrong thing, and I tried to cover.) "I trust you, John. Show some trust in me."

"Look," he hesitated . . . then plunged, "I'll tell you what is done when a stranger stumbles onto Sunnyview. Okay? I'll tell you if you promise me two things. First, you let me explain without interruption and second, when I finish you ask no questions and/or no further explanation, elaboration, or details. Deal?"

"Deal," I said, and raised my glass ritually. He began, talking slowly and carefully, enunciating his words to emphasize the fact that he wasn't going to repeat himself.

"First off, the stranger is treated kindly, with courtesy and generosity. We feed him or her, or them, and administer medical treatment when necessary. In answer to the questions of where they are, we tell them 'a hospital,' nothing more."

I opened my mouth about to speak, but John simply held up his palm in a gesture to halt me, and continued: "If, during the course of preliminary interviews, we determine that our stranger has no strong ties at home, or no home at all, and he possesses a skill or talent we could employ, he is . . . he is subtly made aware of the opportunity to stay."

"Nicely put," I commented. John allowed a perceptible nod of acknowledgment without pause.

"Having become aware that he can stay, either he will ask us if he may do so, or depending on how badly we need his particular skill, we may ask him. If there is mutual agreement that he will join us, he enters into a program of orientation and education. Okay?" It was a rhetorical "Okay" and the saint moved onward. "If . . . if, however, this trespasser . . ." (I smiled cynically at the change in nomenclature, but the saint's expression remained sober.) ". . . If our stranger wants out, wants to go back where he came from, wants to go home or whatever, if he wants to leave Sunnyview, we lie."

"Aha," I interrupted in minor triumph.

"Aha, your holier-than-thou self." He was irritated, which is to say, relative to the saint's temperament, enraged.

He continued. "We explain that Sunnyview is a government hospital and its whereabouts are top secret. Having explained that, we further explain to them that they must undergo a treatment that will erase the memory of their ever being here but will not harm them in any way. If they refuse such treatment and insist on leaving, we accomplish the treatment by subterfuge. A doctored cup of coffee, or whatever, to render them amiable. In any case, no one leaves Sunnyview with the memory of their being here still intact. It is vital to our purpose that we remain isolated, and our location and very existence an airtight secret."

"But," I began, about to ask the first of four-hundred questions.

"But," said John, cutting me off and raising his glass in a mock toast, "of course you are a man of your word and you'd like another beer."

"Another beer," I agreed impotently. John smiled.

"You," he said, "are not one of those strangers. You are not an accident, Seb." Which, of course, was my first question.

We had lunch and idled away still another hour or two over several cups of coffee, talking about golf and other things relevant to nothing. I interrupted the trivia once to make a call at a dialless public phone in a half booth near the men's room. The operator was able to connect me with Dr. Manna. I told him strongly that I wished to see him as soon as possible and he replied as kindly and sweetly as ever that I was scheduled to see him at 9 A.M. the following day. He added, less than ominously, that we were going to have a very long talk this time.

From the clubhouse John and I meandered across the grounds to the dorm. Somehow I managed to kill what was left of the day. I played several games of chess with the saint, who proved to be quite formidable, and I ended the evening seated near the fireplace in the Winter room in a giant velours chair, listening to Beethoven. I was plucked from my reverie by the scent of delicious perfume and the rustle of a dress.

"He's perennial, isn't he?" It was Kelly Green, standing by my side, gazing into the hearth that rosed her milky skin.

75

"Beethoven?" I asked, then answered tritely, "As the grass."

She was one of those rare redheads who is genuinely beautiful. It's sad and, I suppose, cruel, but most women who are blessed with red hair are also gifted with beet-red skin and/or buck teeth. This beauty who stood by the fire had no such flaws.

"What is your name so that I won't call you 'Red?' "

"I like to be called Red."

"You do?"

"I do." She smiled a marvelous eyes-only smile and sat at my feet with a sudden graceful move, resting her cheek against my thigh and holding my leg like a child. Just like that.

An incredibly tactless question popped into my mind and was as quickly out of my mouth.

"Where is Julie?—I'm sorry." I added quickly, "That was dumb." She rolled her head to rest the other cheek against my thigh, facing me.

"No, it wasn't," she said, glowing up at me. "Julie's on duty tonight. That's why I'm here."

I stroked her hair and she lifted her head and smiled and turned again to face the fire. The movement covered my lap with her red-gold tresses and she hugged my leg. The total effect was a gesture of loving submission . . . milk and honey to the male ego, and therefore enchantingly captivating. Within minutes she was in my room and in my bed and in my arms. She was extraordinary.

Kelly Green—Red—departed from my lair furtively in the night, and just as well, for this day was a day of man-talk and appropriate action. It was macho time and, as all warriors know, one cannot serve Eros while serving Mars. I wanted all the answers from that bastard Bananas and I wanted them that morning. I snapped from bed to bathroom like a Marine, urinated violently, and brushed my teeth with controlled fury.

I trooped downstairs to the dining room and energized myself with two eggs over easy (would that they served toasted hobnails), gulped down two cups of black coffee to wire my nerve endings, checked the time, and at 0850 headed for Field Marshall Bananas's office in a straight, unrelenting march.

"Come in, Sebastian. Sit down. How are you this morning?"

"I want to get all the answers. All of them, today . . . now," I gritted.

"And high time, I should think," he said pleasantly. "And so you shall. Coffee?"

"Yes, thank you. Black with a little sugar." He poured from an electric percolator hooked up at the bar at the rear of the office. Not into common mugs, of course, but cups and saucers of a delicate china, which he placed on the coffee table between the two black Naugahydes.

He made three trips between the bar and the coffee table. First, with the two cups of coffee in their saucers, inviting me to be seated and to make myself comfortable; then, with a small pitcher of cream and a small silver bowl of lump sugar; and, finally, the mandatory touch—he opened a box of cigars to set his scene exactly.

"Cigar, Sebastian?" he asked, moving Queen's pawn two spaces.

"Yes." I withdrew a cigar, sniffed it, and nipped the end. He may have been in a chess-playing mood but mine was more suitable to a rugby scrum. I fixed my eyes on him and, instead of removing the snipped tobacco in a gentlemanly manner from my tongue tip, I spit it out vulgarly merely to disturb him. It didn't. I accepted a light, stirred a lump of sugar into my coffee, sipped it, placed it back in its saucer, and silently puffed on the richly dark cigar without taking my eyes from his.

"Have you thought of some specifics, Sebastian? The fact that you want to know *all* the answers expresses your desire to come out of the dark, as it were—and I can understand your feelings—but it will be easier, I think, if you ask me questions and I answer them detailed to your satisfaction. Do you agree?"

I decided on a broadside to try to rumple his aristocratic effect just a smidgen.

"You strike me as a no-good son-of-a-bitch who is probably as honest as a hungry crow. What can you say up front to convince me at all that your answers will not be at best half truths and at worst continued expedient lying. Saint John admitted that you people had a kind of malleable ethic when dealing with strangers."

"But you, Sebastian, as John told you, are not a stranger. You were *brought* to Sunnyview. You didn't stumble on us." He sat back and puffed on his cigar. "Relax, Sebastian. Take your time. Enjoy your coffee and your cigar, and I will answer your questions."

"All right," I said. "Why am I here? Why are you here? What is your purpose and what do you want of me?"

"You are here because you were sick and we wanted to make you well."

He rose from his chair, strolled to the window, and assumed his Napoleon-in-the-sunlight stance, but this time there was something convincing in the air.

"Do you know the Hippocratic Oath, Sebastian? Not the exact words, of course, but could you paraphrase it? Most people," he said, without waiting for an answer, "most people would paraphrase it something like: 'I promise to treat my patients to the best of my ability and never to refuse to treat them, so help me

God.'" He held his cigar mockingly over his heart. "Something on that order, no?

"Not on your life, my dear Sebastian. A misconception; one of many regarding Hippocrates.

"Hippocrates's legacy was to elevate the doctor from half trickster, half priest, to scientist. To raise his profession to an art and, most important, to introduce brotherhood to the practice of medicine." With that he turned to the wall of books and, after a moment of scanning, extracted a small text, which he ruffled through until he found what he hunted. He then mumbled down the page, turned it, and commenced to read aloud to me with an upraised index finger emphasizing the alleged importance of the words.

I will look upon him who shall have taught me this art as one of my parents. I will share my substance with him, and I will supply his necessities, if he be in need. I will regard his offspring even as my own brethren, and I will teach them this art, if they would learn it, without fee or covenant. I will impart this art by precept, by lecture, and by every mode of teaching, not only to my own sons but to the sons of him who has taught me, and to disciples bound by covenant and oath, according to the law of Medicine.

Dr. Manna snapped the book shut with one hand and replaced it, then turned and announced melodramatically: "Since the time of Hippocrates we have been at war—a war against the ignorant who regard scientific enlightenment as the work of the devil. Our weapon . . . our supreme weapon . . . was allegiance, not to mankind, but to each other. This allegiance grew in strength as time after time we saw the deadly fickle nature of man in action against us. We saw men fall to their knees in homage to our miracles and drag us to the heretics' stake for presenting a new truth. A doctor's family, Sebastian, his only real family, is his fellow physicians. His God, his only God is Truth." He looked at his watch and abruptly announced it was time for lunch.

"What do you think of Freud, Sebastian?" he asked as he walked me, arm around my shoulder, to the door.

"In how many words?"

He smiled. "We can talk some more if you'd like after lunch."

"I'll be here." I said.

6.

I was very hungry, but I opted for aimless strolling rather than heading straight for the dorm and the scheduled fried chicken lunch.

He didn't say much, I thought. All the business about Hippocrates and the need for blood oath loyalty among medical men was interesting but it was obviously just the foundation he was laying for a much more revealing structure.

As I walked, I rolled the interview over in my mind, listened carefully, rewound it, and rolled it again, analyzing every phrase, looking for subtleties of meaning, only to discover what every actor knows—that the truth behind words is as diverse as the infinite number of inflections available to the human voice. And Bananas was a cool one, he was. The slogan "Never put bananas in the refrigerator" popped to mind and I smiled my way out of my daydream to discover my meandering had brought me to the front door of the dorm and the stomach-grumbling-inducing smell of fried chicken. When I got to the dining room, I efficiently ordered from a waitress en route to a vacant table.

I soon found myself happily at work devouring half a hen that was delicious. Sunnyview, I mused, had advanced to the outer limits in the art of chicken cookery.

"Who's been starving you?"

I looked up slowly because I knew who it was. The legs.

"Julie. How are you? Long time no see," I said, with controlled nonchalance.

"Been working," she smiled. "May I?" She pulled back the chair with her question, sat, propped her chin on her hands, and stared at me in a way that was less disconcerting than nerve-racking.

"How was Kelly Green?" she asked plainly.

"How did you ...?"

"She told me you called her that name all night long. She told you she liked to be called Red, Sebastian."

"She told you a lot."

"Why not?" Her smile grew broader.

I was suddenly aware that a grease stained napkin and a plate of chicken bones was less than appropriate for a love scene, and I signaled for a girl to clear the table.

"How about a walk, Julie?"

"No," she said, and pointed over my shoulder, "I have to be back on the floor at one and it's a quarter to."

I turned to glance at the clock she indicated, then back to her with a nod of resignation. A girl came to clear the table and we leaned back to afford her intrusion, then forward again after the last bothersome wipe.

"Tonight, Julie?"

"Tonight," she said, "I'm back on the day shift."

The footing slipped out from under my mind as I felt myself being sucked back to the nightmare world of those first few weeks. Day shift . . . night shift . . . I could see the wild eyes of those dark nurses as they drank their evil cups dry in the glow of the dark lamp. Was I insane at the time? Was I still?

"What's wrong, Seb? You're white as a sheet."

"When you said 'day shift' it reminded me . . ."

"Oh, that. You were hallucinating then, Seb. I know, I was there. Remember?"

"I remember, but you're *real*. How were you part of it? I don't understand." I reached out and clasped her hand with both of mine. "I don't know where reality stops and where it begins."

"You're in reality now, darling; you're sure

of that, aren't you?" She brought her free hand to mine and squeezed.

"I guess. I guess so, Julie."

"You've been through a lot, baby. Can I come to your room tonight and comfort you?"

She smiled, knowing the question was rhetorical. She gave my hand a parting squeeze and rose from her chair. She crossed the room and walked to the exit accepting admiring stares as she went with the hauteur of a princess ... or a sorceress.

People began shuffling things, making the classroom sounds of five to the hour and I shook myself out of my reverie. It was time to return to Bananas and Chapter Two—Freud, he had said.

In minutes I had crossed the grounds and was standing outside Bananas' lair. I hesitated a long moment, with my hand poised to knock, when I heard his voice. Not from within the office, but from behind me.

"Have a good lunch, Sebastian?"

I turned my head, one hand still poised on doorknob and the other hand fisted to knock, somehow transfixed in that increasingly dumb posture.

"You may turn the knob, Sebastian," he smiled. "No locks—remember?"

I opened the door and walked in, thinking how foolishly I was behaving.

"Coffee? Wine?" he threw over his shoulder

as he walked to the bar at the far side of the office. "What's your poison?"

"You mean what's my drug."

He paused at the bar and turned to me. "No, Sebastian, no drugs. Just plain coffee, plain wine. I promise."

"I'll just take another of these cigars," I said, reaching for the box of the coffee table.

"If we were of a mind to drug you, Sebastian," he said, while pouring himself some white wine, "we could as easily do so with cigars."

"Do you have mice in your pocket?"

"I beg your pardon?"

"I said, do you have mice in your pocket? Or is that the divine 'we?'"

"It is the collective 'we,' Sebastian; the collective 'we.'"

I plunked down in what seemed to have become *my* chair, and lit my Panatela.

"I believe you, Doctor. I'm just too full for anything more oral than a cigar. In any case, you're quite right. You could get drugs in me with an infinite variety of means. So, therefore, I will take your word."

He smiled.

"We left off at Sigmund Freud, Doctor."

"So we did," he said, raising his glass to me in praise of my earnestness. "Freud, Sigmund Freud," almost to himself, then to both of us: "A man of such public impact that his name became part of our language, used to describe a way of thinking. Freudian." Then turning to me fully, "Do you think a derivative of my name will wind up in the dictionary, Sebastian?"

"It already has," I said, and his eyebrows arched over his wine glass waiting my response.

"Maniac," I said.

The smile grew broader in response to my little joke, but in a way that was chilling because it did not become more animated or happier. I decided that Bananas had not a sense of humor . . . not a bit. He could only smile, I fancied, because he could observe how it's done, and his smile was a contrived appropriate gesture, not a gut reaction to feelings. Bananas had to turn to the window with a feigned show of interest in a passing nurse to avoid letting the smile disfigure his face. That's what a faked smile does, you know; if held too long it grows grotesque.

There was a bit of silence as he stood, back to me, at the window. "Oh," he said, raising his wine with a pointed finger in the air denoting a just-thought-of thought, "did you get a kit?"

"Yes," I answered.

"Good," he said, but he had seen the kit plainly on my belt before, and this was just a little interlude he manufactured to blur away my maniac remark. The phony son-of-a-bitch.

"Freud." I prompted.

"Ah yes, Freud. Freud and the alleged monumental innovation of psychoanalysis."

"Not monumental, I gather."

"Sebastian, there has not been in the history of the medical profession a flop, a failure, or disappointment equal to psychoanalysis relative to its expectations. It grew and blossomed and burgeoned in all directions. Millions of textbooks were written, published, and pored over by thousands of medical students who labored to become psychiatrists and who took up lances to the dragon—mental illness—like so many pipe-smoking chair-bound Quixotes. They came, they saw, they blew their smoke rings."

"But you said Freud's theories were right."

Glass of wine still in hand, he took the chair opposite me. "They were, Sebastian. I'm not saying all his theories were wrong. I'm not even saying that some of his theories were entirely wrong. I *am* saying that what we did with them was equivalent to discovering electricity and then trying to light cities with lightning rods. Right solution, wrong application. Or perhaps I should rightfully say, half a solution and therefore no solution at all."

"I'm sorry, Doc, I don't follow you."

"Statistics were compiled, Sebastian, of people undergoing various forms of psychotherapy. The results showed about one-third got better, about one-third got worse, and about one-third were unaffected."

"So?"

"Surveys were taken of people with similar problems who did *not* undergo therapy."

"And?"

"One-third got better, one-third got worse, one-third were unaffected. The results were the same for those who underwent treatment as those who did not. The only difference was that doctors wrote voluminous case history books about those who improved *because* of therapy and thusly built a temple to Freud that stood for years until we began to look hard at the statistics."

"I see . . . I think."

"But Freud had grasped, if not discovered, a fundamental and obvious formula, and it is this:

"All action is based on motivation.

"All motivation is based on experience.

"Experience is memory.

"It is simplicity itself."

He shifted on his buttocks, uncrossing his legs and recrossing them. Once again comfortable, he continued.

"Did you know, Mr. Cant, that many cultures, some on this continent, would use round logs to move great stones, yet never used carts or wagons? They dragged material and belongings along the ground on inefficient sleds, overcoming friction with their sweat, or with draft animals, if lucky. Why? If they used logs that were selected for roundness to move large stones, *that* was the wheel, was it not? So why inefficient sleds instead of wagons?"

"I'll bite. Why?"

"Because the wheel was not the great invention." His eyes narrowed. "The great invention was the stationary axle. It was the stationary axle that begat the airplane. The wheel rolled, but the axle carried.

"Freud gave us the wheel. Half the solution. To illustrate, let us take a Hollywood scenario of a psychotic killer. We see a man outside a schoolyard. He is looking at little girls. We see by his furtive actions, the upturned collar, etcetera, that he is a child molester. As the movie progresses he is caught, arrested, and a liberal-minded judge rules in favor of hospitalization. He is lying on a couch and talking aimlessly and the therapist drops his handkerchief. The camera zooms in. We see the man's sweating face and we zoom back to the handkerchief, which becomes a shawl and back to the man and the scene fades back to his childhood."

I smiled at Bananas's enthusiasm, which irritated him.

"You *do* want to understand, don't you, Sebastian?"

"I'm sorry . . . yes."

"Well, the point is; in the typical Hollywood treatment the man would dredge from his mind some awful experience from his childhood, recognize the connection to his abnormal deviation, and thusly be cured. All that was left was the closing scene showing him walking free and then the credit crawl."

"Not so?"

"Not so at all, Mr. Cant. Case history after case history proved that such deviated behavior persisted. But digging out the causative memories was part of the solution. That was the wheel."

"And the axle?"

"That, Sebastian, is obvious."

"Destroy the memory?"

"Not the entire memory. Just the particular experience that is the root cause of the unwanted behavior."

"You mean just reach in and pluck out the specific memory you don't like and extinguish it?"

"Precisely. As easily as one erases a tape on a recorder."

"You can't do that," I said, but his smile refuted the statement and enormity of what he was alleged stunned me silent.

"If you could speak, Sebastian, I think your next question would be *how*?"

I nodded dumbly.

"Do you see why I have taken pains to educate you gradually? Do you see, as one sees the tip of the iceberg, the profundity of what we are accomplishing at Sunnyview? The awesome power for benevolence we have in our control?"

"An iceberg," I said when at last I gained use of my voice, "is not benevolent, Doctor Manna."

"Merely a metaphor, Sebastian. Perhaps ill chosen."

"Perhaps, Doctor, it was—what is the phrase?—a Freudian slip."

He smiled but his eyes were made of stone.

7.

AFTER leaving Bananas's office it seemed
like I fell into a semitrance and somnambulated
my way to the dorm and thence to the Winter
room fireplace, where I kept a girl in blue busy
seeing my wine glass was full. The saint came in
and, since my boozy attention was on the fire,
he was at my shoulder before I saw him.

"How'd it go today, Seb?"

"Not bad," I said without turning. "Interesting place you got here, Saint John. Only
Sunnyview is a poor choice for a name. It
ought to be called . . ." I drank my wine.

"It ought to be called what, Seb?"

I flung the glass crashing into the fireplace
and spit my reply. "How about Hotel Amnesia,
or . . . or . . ."

"Take it easy, Seb."

I stood before the hearth with my hands on
my hips, shaking, and when I turned my head

to the saint I saw in back of him startled firelit faces staring. "What the hell are you looking at?" I yelled. I flailed my arms and magically all the faces clicked off as the onlookers gave the backs of their heads to me and the firelight.

"Sit down, please, Seb." John was asking nicely while forcing me into the chair.

"I'm sorry . . . no, I'm not sorry. That bastard . . ." My voice started to rise again and I controlled it to a lower level of intensity in deference to the Saint's pleading gestures to act at least partially civilized. ". . . that bastard, this hospital, has taken part of my memory, hasn't it? I mean he practically told me that today. That's what you do here, isn't it? You operate on the brain to take away memory, right? Or part of it. Listen, I am goddamn mad, Saint. I am bloody angry. What right does anyone have to . . . I mean that is like altering the soul itself. I mean if you destroy a man's memory totally, you've destroyed his soul. I'm leaving here, John. No shit, I am leaving!"

John looked away and I panicked. I grabbed a fistful of his lapel and shirt front and pulled him down to me. "Hey, Seb, leggo!" He held his voice to a rasping whisper and pushed at my hand.

"Why did you look away when I said I was leaving?"

"I was trying to think of what to say."

"What do you mean, John?" I still held him fast.

"I mean you've jumped to too many conclusions." He had put both hands on my closed fist and was pushing so hard I had to release him or take his shirt front. "Thank you, friend," he said. He straightened his clothes facing the fire, and I glanced around to see the disembodied heads look quick and turn away. Sunnyview was not used to violence. With a gesture of his head toward our ogling audience, John suggested we sample the night air. It was a timely and proper idea. Once outside, though, I resumed my harangue as we walked aimlessly along the winding paths.

"That sort of thing is not right, John."

No comment.

"Certain things are inviolate."

No comment.

"The ends do not justify the means . . . always."

No comment.

"I can't stand it, John."

"What?"

"Your incessant babbling."

A smile.

"Wait a little longer, Seb."

"Wait for what?"

"A little more explanation. You only know a small part, not enough to make a judgment.

Today is Thursday. You'll see Dr. Manna every day for this next week. By Wednesday you should have it all. Wait until then, okay, old buddy?"

"It's going to be a long weekend, John."

"What weekend?"

"Saturday and Sunday, of course. Or, are you saying I'll see Bananas on those days?"

John turned and with his arm on my shoulder spun me gently around toward the dorm and we started back.

"We have no weekends here at Sunnyview. Why should we?"

Of course, why should they? In a moment we were back at the dorm entrance.

At first I wasn't sure whether she was behind me, reflected in the glass door I faced, or standing inside the foyer. John opened the door and the image did not move with it.

"Hi, Julie."

"Hi, John. Hello, Seb."

"Hello."

"My, we look solemn," she said.

"Cheer him up, Julie, he's not much of a sport tonight." John started into the Winter room, leaving us in the foyer, but stopped and turned for a last admonition. "You'll wait a week, Seb? You won't try to . . ."

"No, I'll wait, John. My word."

"Okay," he said, disappearing.

I turned to Julie, who took my hand and led

me back outside. We walked down a gray path out to the openness of the gray rolling lawns, and as the lights of the dorm grew distant the heavens grew dazzlingly starry bright. Her hand in mine was smooth and warm and her hair blew lightly.

"Are you troubled, Seb?"

"Reading my mind?"

"No, Seb, feeling your feelings would be more correct. Let's sit, the grass is warm."

"Electronically."

She ignored the sourness of my tone and pulled me down to sit with her, and when I sat she gently drew my head to rest on her lap. I turned on my back and held her hand, looking up into and beyond the infinite stars, letting them swallow me in their vastness.

"There is a promise up there," I said. "A memory of other times, of other worlds that once were and will be again. A memory locked somewhere in our genes, and not far below our consciousness. It's wrong to screw with the memory, Julie." She stroked my forehead and said nothing beyond an acquiescent uh-huh. I twisted and strained my neck around to look up at her. "I mean it, Julie. The memory is the soul. It is the essence of a man's life. It is inviolate." I allowed my neck to relax back to a more comfortable position, resting my chin on my chest.

"It is wrong to destroy memory, and that's what's been done to me."

"Has it?" She continued to stroke my forehead and twist ringlets of my hair in her fingers.

"Damn right." I sat up abruptly and turned to face her. "Bananas as much as told me that, in today's interview." She rested back on her palms.

"He did? Or he *as much as* did?"

"Well, he said that they . . . funny, I guess you are included when I say *they* . . ." She shook her hair, not in a negative response, but merely one of those pointless gestures peculiar to females. "He is able to erase memories," I continued, "apparently with the same ease as one erases a tape on a recorder. As a matter of fact, that is the exact analogy Bananas used. Well, the fact is that there are certain gaps in my own memory; mostly about my job and my immediate past, prior to coming here . . . or being brought here, which is more the truth."

"Two and two make four, is that your logic, Seb?"

"As a matter of fact, they do don't they? Are you denying what I suggest? Are you saying that my memory has not been tampered with?"

"No."

"Are you then affirming that it has?"

"No."

"You are bloody well then playing games, and I'm in no mood for it."

I got to my feet and slapped the grass from my trouser seat. She tucked her legs under her, like a young girl, and said as plaintively, "Don't go, Seb."

"Are you a purposeful distraction, Julie?" I said with meanness.

"Please," she said, and extended her hand while still maintaining the pose. I took her hand and she smiled and I allowed myself to be drawn down to her again, and I kissed her and the meanness left.

"I love you, Seb."

I held her away by her shoulders. "What kind of love is it when you ask me if I enjoyed being with another woman while you were busy? What kind of love is that?"

"Not possessive love, Seb. Is possessive love true love? Isn't it much truer, much more selfless, to want the object of your love to be happy, to be pleasured?"

"No."

"No?"

"Not pleasured by someone else."

She lay back and gently pulled me down with her until she was lying flat with her arms around my neck and I was supported by my hands over her. I gave way to her arms, and gravity, and the Lord God Eros, and in

99

moments we were making delicious love on the warm grass.

Very little was said during the remainder of the evening. We returned to the dorm and sipped wine, and stared into each other's eyes, and finally went to my room and to bed.

I was just drifting off to sleep when suddenly I was wide awake and sitting bolt upright.

"He said *try*," I announced to no one.

"What is it, darling?" Julie sat up and put her arm over my bare shoulder, "What is it, Seb?"

"Saint John said *try*."

"I don't understand, Seb," she said sleepily, "lie down, honey." I shifted around to face her.

"When John was leaving us tonight in the foyer, he asked me to promise not to *try*, and before he finished I said I wouldn't. That he had my word. Remember? I knew the end of his sentence was try to escape."

"I suppose . . ."

"But he said *try*, Julie, that means attempt. Why would he say try to leave if I could in fact leave any time I wanted?"

"I'm sure it was a slip of the tongue."

"Yes, I'll bet!"

She sat straighter and fluffed her hair. "You saw for yourself that when you took off running that day no one stopped you, Seb. You laughed at yourself, remember?"

100

"Then why did he say 'try,' Julie? The one factor that has kept me from panicking was the security that I could leave Sunnyview any time I chose to. Do you understand? The thought that I might be a prisoner here turns my intestines cold. I cannot stand the feeling of being trapped. It's a claustrophobic thing."

"You're not trapped, Seb. You're free to go any time. Please lie back and go to sleep. Don't panic over a single word. Please?"

I didn't answer but I lay back slowly, and her arms crept around me, and I somehow pushed the fear from my mind and I drifted into sleep.

"Welcome, welcome, welcome, little tiny Sebastian Cant!"

"You have no right whatsoever to take my ba-ba," I said, as I wagged my finger at Dr. Manna for emphasis. He had on the black robe of a judge and was seated high on a judge's bench. I wagged my finger, absolutely outraged at the obvious injustice of the allotted sizes. I, for instance, was either no more than four inches high, or the enormous black Naugahyde easy chair I was seated on was at least fifteen to twenty feet in width. In either case, the effect was the same. I looked ludicrously small and thus ineffectual.

This state of affairs was obviously engineered by the prosecution, I thought. Crafty fellows who would stop at nothing. I lowered myself over the edge of the chair, hung a moment, and dropped to the floor, a good twelve feet below, twisting my ankle in the process. Limping, I approached the bench and, cupping my hands round my mouth, I yelled up at the judge, "I object!"

"On what grounds?" he thundered.

"I beg the court's pardon!" I yelled back with my hand to my ear, feigning deafness to gain time to think.

"On what grounds?" he screamed, and pounded the gavel like Thor. The ground beneath my feet trembled, but I formulated my objection and yelled up at the bench,

"On the grounds of *nolo contemptuous!*"

There was much shifting about and furtive murmuring by the D.A. and his quiet, ugly assistant. This was a move they obviously did not expect. At last, the D.A. (the black mustachioed bastard) spoke.

"This, Your Honor, is another of Sebastian Cant's cheap courtroom tricks. It is irrelevant and unbearable!"

"Objection sustained!" said Bananas.

"Your Honor," I said, and wiped the nape of my neck with a large white handkerchief, "because of the hot, sticky weather, I move that the clerk open the windows."

"So ordered!" He motioned to the bailiff, who lowered the top half of the windows with a long pole. People in the audience clapped here and there in response to this move. Southerners were quite a friendly lot, I mused.

"Your Honor, I would like to call my first and only witness." I allowed a moment to sip from a glass of water for dramatic effect, "and *that* witness is me!"

Suddenly the courtroom was boiling over with a mixture of cheers and catcalls, and the camp of the prosecution was in total disarray.

"Your Honor!" The D.A. was on his feet, sweaty and fat and nervous. "I object!"

"On what grounds?"

"This is another of Sebastian Cant's cheap courtroom tricks. It is without precedent in the annals of criminal and other justice!"

"You have a point, Mr. Prosecutor. Will both counsels approach the bench, please?" We did.

"Your Honor!" I yelled up. He leaned on the bench and looked down at me, squinting.

"Speak louder, Mr. Cant, I can hardly hear you."

"That's one of the things *I* object to, Your Honor. Why are the D.A. and his ugly assistant six feet tall while I'm only four inches?"

Bananas thought for a moment, then turned to the jury box.

"The jury is instructed to disregard the laughable size of the defendant and his lawyer, who are one and the same."

Only a minor victory, to be sure, but it set the tone of my defense.

"I should herewith and forthright like to take the stand at this time, and answer questions put to myself by me. Any objections, anybody?"

"Any objections?" the judge annoyingly echoed.

"No," said the D.A.

"I don't give a shit." said his ugly assistant.

"I shall ask myself questions by means of a tape recorder which I shall place on the black Naugahyde easy chair and control by this remote control device I hold in my very hand. Any objections, anyone?"

"No objections," chorused the D.A., his assistant, and Bananas.

I mounted the witness chair, which I found to be of my size, and it was only then that I noticed that the jury members were all my height, which I judged to be another factor in my favor. I pressed the remote control button, and the machine seated on the easy chair clicked and hummed. Then my voice, recorded earlier, crackled out the first question.

"What is your name, occupation, and room?"

"Sebastian Cant, lawyer and defendant, corner room, second floor." I pressed the button again.

"Where are you?" the machine asked. I

shifted. This was a question I did not remember taping.

"I didn't ask that question, Your Honor." The D.A. and his ugly assistant were on their feet at once.

"We object! This is one more clever courtroom trick by Sebastian Cant."

"The defendant is directed to answer the question," ordered the judge. I was trapped, I thought, by my own recorder.

"I am at Sunnyview," I answered, growing nervous. I pressed the button again.

"What about before?" asked the machine. I leapt to my feet.

"What the hell kind of question is that?"

"Order! Order!" thundered Bananas. His voice and his huge pounding gavel were deafening. I cupped my hands to my ears, fearful my eardrums would burst.

"Please, Your Honor, don't pound that gavel."

"We demand he answer the question he just asked himself," yelled the D.A. gleefully.

"Order! Order!" pounded Thor, and I knew I had to answer or the noise would kill me. My ears were trickling blood into my hands.

"I don't remember about before," I pleaded.

"That is no answer, Your Honor," said the ugly assistant. "It's another trick."

"It's the only answer I have, Your Honor."

Bananas leaned over and smiled down at me.

His teeth were large and yellow. "Go on, Mr. Cant, the court accepts your answer since it is, after all, your question." I pressed the button again.

"What about before?" asked the machine. I pressed the button again quickly. "What about before?" it asked again.

"You have to answer now!" yelled the D.A. "You asked three times. That's the law . . . California Penal Code 3069234."

"He has to answer!" screamed the ugly assistant, all the while jumping up and down, pulling out his white hair by the handful, and throwing it at me.

"Order! Order!" and Bananas's voice was shaking the floor under me. He raised to his towering height and pounded his sledgehammer gavel on the oak bench, thundering, thundering, with such exploding volume that both my ears fell off into my cupped hands and I held them out, matted and dripping blood.

"Sebastian, Sebastian." It was Julie. I woke up soaked to the skin and icy cold.

8.

BANANAS smiled: "Just a dream."

"Like hell! Another of your drug-induced nightmares, that's what it was." I was shaking head to toe.

"Just a dream, Seb."

"Don't call me Seb, Doctor, and don't bull-shit me."

"After our talk today, Mr. Cant, you will see that it would not make sense for us to induce a dream such as the one you describe."

"You say that as if you could control the substance of a dream. I can accept that you may be able to drug me to produce a nightmare, but I'm sure I'm the only one who can write the scenario. You cannot do that."

"We can indeed write the scenario, as you put it." He smiled. He was telling the truth.

"Then did you? Did you induce that nightmare I had last night?"

107

"In a word, no. Coffee?"

"It was just a spontaneous nightmare?"

"Cream? Sugar?" He had answered no, and obviously was not going to expound.

"One lump. Black. You're a real sweetheart, Bananas."

He smiled. But it was perceptibly forced. He didn't like that nickname one whit.

"You don't care for the name Bananas, Bananas?"

He brought over two cups in their blue saucers to the coffee table and set one delicately before me. His hands trembled slightly with restrained anger. "I'll make a pact with you, Mr. Cant. You refrain from calling me that nickname you think so funny, and I'll not call you Seb, as you requested. Fair?"

This was delightful. He couldn't even bring himself to say Bananas, it disturbed him so much. That is the burden of these larger than God types, I thought. Their egos are so bloody fragile.

"No. Not fair, Bananas."

He was genuinely surprised. He thought his mere suggestion was an agreement. The egotistical bastard.

He put his cup and saucer down with such abruptness it spilled.

"Look here, Sebastian, I don't wish to play games! I am a doctor. I hold licenses and scholastic degrees that entitle me to that appellation. You will cease at once calling me that insulting name, or I will ... I will ..."

"Or you will what, Doctor? Operate on me and destroy my memory totally? Is that your threat?" As the words spilled out, I saw in his blank nondenial expression that I might be voicing a truth and my stomach sank. I back-pedalled in panic.

"Aw, look, what's the point? I'm sorry, Doctor. I admit it, I was just trying to get your goat. You're right, I'm just wasting both our time, and you are in fact a doctor and entitled to respect." As I spoke, my mouth became drier. It was the man's silence that scared me. All egomaniacs with power are dangerous as hell and you dare not puncture their self-image. You daren't ridicule. In the eyes of a Schicklgruber nothing about him is subject to humor. I wet my throat with coffee.

"Please accept my apology, Doctor, and go on. I am really anxious to learn. I hope you understand my fearfulness about the awful nightmare I had." I wet my throat again and placed my cup back in its saucer.

"That's all right, Sebastian, I understand." He walked back to the bar, where he retrieved a small rag and brought it back to the table to mop up the spilled coffee.

"I realize you've been under a strain," he said, apparently satisfied by my display of submission and fear.

"Yes sir," I said, "I'm glad you understand."

Having mopped dry the spilt coffee, he took the rag back to the bar and dumped it behind, presumably in a sink. He then returned to the chair opposite me and resumed his discourse.

"I have told you, Sebastian, that we can destroy memory. Do you believe me?"

"I don't know."

"Let me give you a brief education regarding memory functionings and then I will explain how it is possible."

"Shoot."

"First off, there are two memories. Short term and long term. In order to make a short-term memory long term we can employ devices such as repetition. In order to retrieve from the bank of long-term memory we can deposit these thoughts and ideas along with associations. Memory experts employ this device. Traumatic memories can be retrieved by exploiting the associations deposited with the trauma. Secondly, once a memory is retrieved it is then easy to recall when needed. It is in long term but no longer lost in the subconscious. But how exactly is memory stored? How is it physically retained in the brain? No one had the answer to this.

"The breakthrough, Sebastian—turning point is perhaps a better phrase—came with the work of a somewhat unorthodox psychologist named James McConnell and his experiments with the lowly flatworm. These flatworms, called Planarians, were taught, by McConnell, to react to light, a noteworthy feat in itself. Then, in an effort to prove his conceptualized theory, he chopped up these little worms and fed them to untrained worms. The result? The worms who ate their educated cousins learned to react to light much more rapidly than a control group.

"McConnell's theories were treated as a joke, and fellow scientists who tried to replicate his work reported failures. McConnell's thesis was that memory was transferable chemically, and the scientific community involved in brain research divided into two camps, believers and nonbelievers of McConnell's theory."

"You believed," I said.

"I believed."

He sipped his coffee and resumed: "I was frustrated by the possibilities, but it wasn't until I learned of the experiments of another scientist, Dr. Agranoff, that I really became excited.

"Dr. Agranoff trained goldfish to react to light by employing electroshock conditioning. Curious to see if he could increase the ability to retain the training, he injected various chemicals into the brain of the goldfish.

"To his astonishment, Dr. Agranoff found that if he injected Puromycin, a chemical that inhibits the manufacture of protein, into the brain of a newly trained goldfish, the memory of the training was obliterated. He theorized that new protein was required to *fix* a memory and the Puromycin blocked that fixing process." He stood up suddenly. "That, Sebastian Cant, is where the progress in memory control stood when I made *my* discoveries."

"I can hardly wait," I said sarcastically.

He paused to give me an icy stare. He was a cold man, this Manna, and in my mind I redubbed him Dr. Bananastein, with a quiet resolution never to call him that aloud. The icy stare melted and he became more animated. This was *his* part of the epic.

"You see, Sebastian, neurologists had learned that by stimulating the brain with electrodes, experiences sometimes long forgotten would be brought up to the conscious with vivid clarity. Armed with electroencephalographs to measure brain waves, they began mapping the brain by stimulating patients while under local anesthesia. I myself, while operating, had elicited experiences that my patients were later to recall with little difficulty. Having read, in detail, of Agranoff's experiments with his fish, I speculated on the possible results of an injection of Puromycin into the brain immediately after one of these stimulated recollections. Would the memory be retarded? Would it be destroyed altogether?"

"Obviously, you tried your experiment, Doctor. On animals first? Or did you go straight to a human guinea pig?"

"Before I answer that, Sebastian, let me go on a bit further. Short-term memories must be transferred or converted to long-term memory in order to be retained. This, we now know, is a chemical process involving changes in the chemical bases of RNA leading in turn to the formation of memory-retaining proteins. If these proteins are not formed the memory is not locked in long term, and this is the action of forgetting. This is what we do when we look up a number that we know we will call just once and need not remember. The chemical changes in RNA do not take place and the protein is not manufactured. Simple. It is the natural law of conservation at work."

"Conservation?"

"By the law of conservation, Sebastian, I mean that nature never expends unnecessary energy. No volcano ever erupted just for the sake of erupting. The brain does not produce proteins promiscuously to retain unnecessary memories."

"What about traumatic memories?"

"They are perhaps not necessary, but apparently they qualify because of their importance, and this importance is measured by the intensity of impact on the body and mind. A

113

guess might be that such memories are recorded to avoid possible repetition."

"A guess, Doctor?"

"Yes, Sebastian, we are not yet clear as to exactly why a traumatic memory is retained for such long periods since it does not help, but rather, harms. Our *guess* is that it is retained for prevention of repetition, but that conflicts with the fact that it is often repressed in the subconscious."

"In short, you don't know."

"We are not gods, Sebastian."

"I'm relieved," I said.

"To answer your previous question. I first tested my hypothesis on a human, but before you voice any holy indignation, let me point out two things. First, the drug Puromycin is merely an antibiotic, and therefore in itself harmless to human tissue. Secondly, I employed the Puromycin injection in the place of a moderate lobotomy.

"The patient was a girl in her early twenties. She suffered from epilepsy, and her *grand mal* attacks had increased over the years until, at the time of the operation, she was experiencing one almost every day. As was my practice, I experimentally prodded the area to be cut with an electrode and in response the patient began to describe an experience in which she was vomiting in a movie theater. Thoughts of vomiting had preceded nearly all of her *grand*

114

mal attacks. I decided at once to seize this opportunity, and ordered a syringe of 1cc of Puromycin. I injected the antibiotic directly into the tissue area that responded to the electrode. I allowed a minute to pass and stimulated the area again. The patient again visualized herself in a theater but this time she described herself as not feeling good. No mention was made specifically of vomiting. Excited that I was on the right track, I doubled the dosage and injected again. I waited a minute, and again stimulated with the electrode. This time she recalled only being in public and feeling ill, The vividness of her memory was substantially blurred. She no longer saw herself specifically in a movie theater, only 'in public,' and not specifically vomiting but vaguely 'feeling ill.' I elected not to perform the lobotomy, but rather to wait and see if there would be a reduction in the frequency or intensity of her seizure activity. There was. Not a substantial reduction, but a measurable one. Had her seizures, which were increasing in frequency and intensity, just been stabilized, I would have considered the treatment successful, but the intensity had measurably diminished.

"Sure that I was on the right track. I rescheduled the patient for surgery. I repeated the procedure exactly, but increased the dosage to 3ccs of Puromycin. It proved to be lethal.

Since Puromycin was in and of itself nontoxic, I concluded that it was the sheer bulk of the chemical that caused the fatal result."

"Fascinating, Doctor."

"Yes, it is fascinating," he allowed and began pacing again. "Well, this failure, if I could really call it that, only served to whet my determination. I knew, Mr. Cant, I absolutely knew, that my hypothesis was correct, and it was only a matter of finding a chemical *so* powerful that less than 2ccs would inhibit *all* protein production at once."

"Do go on, Doctor." I said leaning forward with a mockery that his ego was blind to.

"Well, to sum up, after nearly two years of daily trial and error, I hit upon a formula that was totally effective. I tested it on over five-hundred rats and, in every case, memory of specific training was totally obliterated when only microscopic amounts were injected into the brain.

"Well?" he said, as he let his hands drop to his sides dramatically.

"Well," I said, "I'll be fucked."

9.

"**T**HEN what happened, Seb?"

"The proceedings were concluded."

"Jeez," prayed John as we walked toward the building that housed the golf course restaurant. "No wonder you greeted me with 'let's get a drink.'"

"Well, I'm sorry, John, what can I say? I couldn't resist. I mean, you should have seen that last poetic pose as he delivered unto me his final victory over memory. It was a mother-in-law bending over presenting her rump, or a second lieutenant ordering 'give me that' when you're holding a chocolate cream pie. Some temptations are beyond human endurance."

"Jeez," he commented.

"Look, Saint, I expect when we climb these stairs and sit to a civilized drink you will have something to say in the way of needed counsel beyond that Brooklynese plea to the Messiah."

117

He was silent and, I hoped, gathering his thoughts toward my problems and their solutions. We mounted barstools, I leading in the choice of seating. There are times for sipping and pleasant reflection. This was a time for hard thinking drinking.

"Whiskey," I ordered, setting the mood properly.

"Two," John amended.

Five drinks later my ranting subdued to mumbling.

"*In vino veritas*," I toasted, and raised my shot glass eye high.

"In booze there is bullshit," countered the saint.

"No. *In vino veritas*, John, for sure."

"And what truth have you espied, Sir Cant?"

"Espause?"

"Espy."

"Espooze." I giggled.

"You will see no truth if you're unconscious, Seb."

"Okay, Okay, Saint John. Dr. Bananastein said . . ."

"Bananastein?"

"As in Frankastein."

"Frankenstein," he corrected.

"You agree, then?"

"I agree it would not be a good idea to call him that to his face." We drank in silence for a while, during which time I managed to put away a number of double shots of Bourbon.

"Listen to me, Saint John." I motioned with my fingers for John to bend closer. I remember at this point I wished to be secretive as only a drunk wishes to be secretive.

"He wants me to be his lab assistant," I whispered.

"His what?"

"Shhh!" I shushed. "He wants me to be his lab assistant and dope up the rats."

Very little of what I said and did after that is clear. With the aid of John Barleycorn I performed my own memory-killing that afternoon, but there is one thing I did remember that proved to be of more than minor importance. John got me to move off the barstool I was riding to oblivion, and guided me to one of the tables at the windowed wall. There he ordered a dinner for both of us, and cajoled me into eating at least part of what was placed before me, his ploy being to sober me with nutritive ingestion. But the food served only to make me sleepy and I suggested we retire. Before we left the table, however, something caught my eye in the knolls just beyond the golf course that spread out before us. It was late afternoon and I had the presence to note the time, which I muddily sensed was a critical item. It was exactly 5:25, when I saw the sun glinting off the shrubbery in a way that indicated something metallic running in more or less a straight line. A fence? Very odd, I thought, and I repeated over in my mind, 5:25, 5:25, 5:25, and noted with concentration the particular table we were seated at—thereby committing these two pieces of information to, saints preserve us, long-term memory.

I succeeded, because, when I awoke, I remembered little of anything that occurred after the beginning of the intense imbibing the day before, save the time, 5:25, and the location of the restaurant seat. The hell of it was, I couldn't recall the importance of these two items or why I felt I needed to remember them.

Scheduled for another interview with that madcap barrel of laughs, Bozo Bananastein, I dressed, ate, and did other things necessary, and plodded with the gaiety of an embalmer to the white building that housed my mentor.

"Good morning, Sebastian."

"*Guten morgen, Herr Doktor.*"

"Ah . . . yes, Sebastian. Please sit down." Pause. "Coffee, Sebastian?"

"Yes."

He smiled his waxen smile, poured us each a cup, and sat to serious business.

"I believe we left off yesterday when I related my discovery of a workable anti-protein followed by your vulgar attempt at humor."

"I wouldn't call it that."

"What would you call it?"

"An appropriate comment. Perhaps a statement of my situation, Doctor, or an historic view of the layman in the scientific world." He ignored this.

"Do you have any questions at this point?"

"A few."

"Go ahead, please." He crossed his legs and folded his arms.

"Why am I here, Doctor?"

"Sebastian, do you recall the story of the man who kidnapped those young girls? The one who burned one of the children in the fireplace to boil out the sin bubbles?"

I'm sure that at that moment my face must have gone quite pale, because Bananastein asked me if I was all right, and reached out his hand in a motion clearly intended to prevent my falling out of the chair in a faint.

"I'm all right," I lied.

"The man is *not* you, Sebastian."

I could feel some of the blood coming back to my brain. The Doctor's assurance that what I was thinking was untrue came not a moment too soon.

"You're right, Doctor. I had imagined it might be me, but if I'm not this Charles L., then what *is* the connection? Or are you drawing some kind of analogy?"

"The method of treatment was the same for

both of you. That is the connection, nothing more . . . except . . ."

"Go on."

"The cause and the cure were the same . . ."

"Go on, Doctor, spill it out."

"The man had a memory, actually a group of memories, all traumatic and associative, that were repressed. You had the same problem only in that you also had a group of infantile experiences, which were repressed and caused violent behavior in later life . . ."

"The treatment was the same," I interrupted, "you operated, and using your anti-protein, erased those memories . . ."

"And eliminated the violent behavior for good and all time," he finished.

"I see."

I sat dumbly trying out my brain. Trying to remember what I could remember. A foolish exercise. He read my knitted brows.

"What are you trying to do, Sebastian? The memory is not like a bunch of file cabinets, that you can objectively look through to see what is missing."

"I suppose. But then—"

"Yes?"

"Why do I have partial memory of things that have been erased?" He sat forward slowly, controlling in vain an obvious stab of anxiety.

"What things, Sebastian?" he asked coolly.

"I can remember, not clearly, but I can remember, my little girl . . . and the window . . . and her blue dress. . ."

The memory was suddenly very real. Very painful. And my eyes began to fill. But I noticed oddly that Bananastein's anxiety had left. He was expressing concern, but he was decidedly more comfortable than a moment before.

"Sebastian, please let me assure you. You may remember part of the night your daughter died, but the violent action that caused her death will never reoccur, and that is what is important."

"What the hell are you talking about? You tell me it's all right that I killed my own child, because it won't happen again?" I buried my head in my hands because I was now crying.

"Sebastian," he laid his hand on my shoulder, "you didn't murder your daughter. There was no intent to kill. You hit her and she ran and the window was open, but you didn't intentionally . . ."

"Thanks, Doc; I'm just a plain old-fashioned child beater who killed accidentally."

"No, no, Sebastian. Your associative reaction was a built-in mechanism that you were no more in control of than your heartbeat. There is no question of guilt or innocence here. And what is more, that associative reaction will never occur again because you are, in fact, cured."

I wiped a wet nose with the back of my hand, which prompted the doctor to produce a handkerchief. "Thanks." I wiped my eyes blood-shot dry and blew my reddened beak.

"Sebastian." Bananastein was abruptly on his feet. "How about a break from the lecture. Would you care to take a stroll with me? I'd like to show you my lab."

"You're still doing research?"

"Still? Still?" He put his arm around my shoulder and headed me toward the door. "Research never ends, Sebastian, it goes on and on as progress goes on, as time goes on." As your mouth goes on, I thought.

In a moment we were in the elevator and falling in humming slow motion.

"Why are laboratories always in the basement, Doctor? Is dank air necessary for experimentation?"

"The quality of the air necessary depends on the experiment," he answered with absolute seriousness.

"I see." The hum stopped. The doors opened. The air was dank. As we de-elevated and walked down the hall with the clicks of our heels resounding off the stone flooring, a phrase to describe this man's obsessiveness angled teasingly in the back of my mind. What the hell was it? As we marched around a corner that presented an interminably long stretch of corridor, I tried to nail the phrase. It described this man's manic need to probe and poke and manipulate just because of the presented power to do so. Why was he so much the antithesis of the poet? The farmer? The fisherman? Why would the act of singing a song be so assuredly alien to him, or for that matter, making love? I could not imagine this iceman engaged in either endeavor.

"Ah, here you are." Bananastein reached beneath his tunic and stretched out a ring of keys on one of those spring-loaded wind-up things. He selected the correct one after two misses, and opened the door. This wasn't a lab. That abbreviation is appropriate to such benign places as college biology classrooms. Bananastein's workshop was more aptly titled by the full appellation, with the accent heavily on the second syllable. This was a laboratory.

The noise was immediate and deafening. All four walls consisted of tiers of cages occupied by chattering simians of varying species. The center of the room was dominated by an operating table, about two feet wide and five feet long. It seemed to be freshly resheeted and recovered at the head with one of those sanitized paper headrests.

Surrounding the table were all manner of machines with panels and viewing copes. To the far side of the operating table stood a midget-sized barber chair, humorous looking save for the menacing leather straps and head-holding apparatus.

"These are my children, Sebastian," he said, and a picture of my own child flooded the screen of my mind. I could see her clearly. Annie . . . just six years old. Her blue dress . . . her blonde hair . . . She was sitting on a redwood bench at a redwood table eating. The picture was frozen. I hung on to it tightly and prayed that it would move so that I could see more. Bananastein was calling me but I tried to shut him out, and hung on to the picture . . . to the memory.

"Sebastian." Bananastein had me by my shoulders. "Sebastian, what's wrong? Do you feel all right?"

"Yes I'm fine. Thank you. I'm fine. I'm Okay." The picture was gone. And I don't think I ever hated anyone in my life like I hated the man who stood before me at that moment.

"Come here, I want to show you something." He was opening a cabinet on the back wall.

"Yes?" I walked across the room to join him. He had withdrawn what looked to be a small walkie-talkie, and was relocking the glass-fronted cabinet. "What is it?" I asked.

"It's a transmitter. Do you recall perhaps reading about a Dr. Delgado, the well-publicized electronic bullfighter?" he continued without a pause for an answer. "Well, that was small potatoes, Sebastian. Primitive by our standards. That bulky apparatus sticking out of the skull of the bull. Compared to where we are now, that was a crystal radio set next to a pocket transistor." He was talking very loudly to make himself heard above the jabbering din of the monkeys. "Watch," he yelled, and holding the face of the transmitter to me he turned a dial. What happened was frightening in its abruptness. Every vocal monkey sound in the room stopped instantly. The animals sat on their haunches and rocked back and forth, or leaned against the walls of their mesh cages as if drunk. The sudden change in the entire demeanor of the room was breathtaking.

"How?" was all I could mumble.

"The pleasure center."

"Oh?" I turned in a slow circle, mesmerized. Every one of the animals looked stoned out of its mind. "They obviously like it."

"For conditioning purposes, it has proven to be far more compelling a reward than either food or sex or, for that matter, even avoidance of pain.

"Rats who learned to stimulate themselves by pressing a lever would do so as much as five thousand times an hour. They would press the lever until they fell in exhaustion; and then after a brief rest they would begin pressing again with equal fervor until once again they dropped with overpowering fatigue. They would choose stimulation of the pleasure center in place of food, to the point of starvation."

"Is that what these monkeys are experiencing now, at this moment?"

"Yes. They feel the stimulation in waves, much like an orgasm, because the stimulation increases and decreases slightly every half second. Now watch this."

Bananastein turned another dial and each of the animals froze perfectly still. They had not been moving about their cages before, to any great extent, but some were rocking, and others were nodding their heads up and down, or running their fingers along the wire mesh walls. When the doctor turned the second dial, they all suddenly became statues with not so much as an eye blink to spoil the effect.

"Are they breathing?"

"Barely. All of their vital functions have slowed considerably."

I looked around the room, and it was chilling indeed. They could all have been stuffed, and that is what one would assume if one had come upon them at that moment.

"Are they still feeling?..."

"You mean are the pleasure centers still being stimulated? No, I have turned that off, and if they were not locked in this catatonic state, you'd know it. They like their stimulation. Fortunately, they are incapable of any protest. I will release them from this control momentarily to allow you to witness their reaction to the stimulation cutoff; but first let me point out a few things."

He walked over to one wall of cages, and I followed. We stopped before a spider monkey standing nearly erect, with his paw fingers protruding through and gripping the mesh; he had been gently rocking back and forth in the raptures of the stimulation, and now he was stark still, his large infant eyes not moving. Bananastein lifted one of the little hairy fingers and it was supple, not muscle-tensed as I had supposed. He clapped his hands together abruptly and loudly in front of those staring eyes, and they did not blink. They were frozen open, and yet at the instant of the sharp hand clap, one could see—or sense—fright in those still eyes. I felt sorry for my little ancestor, but Bananas of course felt nothing but delight at his power over his living toys.

We walked over to a larger, metal barred cage standing by itself in the corner. It celled a magnificent gorilla, about four and a half feet tall, with a huge chest, leaning forward on its knuckles. It too was motionless, but there was something different about the expression in the eyes. Unlike the frightened monkey, the gorilla's bright, tiny eyes were alive with a tense, compacted rage—frightful all the more because it was restrained and sealed.

"Observe, Sebastian, that there are no metal protrusions from the scalp of this or any other specimen in the lab. Look around." It was as he said. The animals in Bananastein's dungeon had nothing attached to any part of their bodies. I asked if they did in fact have electrodes implanted in their brains.

"Look behind the left ear, Sebastian."

I moved to the side of the cage and saw a tiny metal plate barely visible.

"Of course you know enough to understand, Sebastian, that for any transmitting device there must be a receiver. Your friend John Macky told you about the metallic flakes implanted just below the surface of the grass that conduct heat?"

"Yes."

"We have perfected a method of implanting these tiny flakes in the brain in precise locations, treated in such a way as to react to a radio signal of a specific frequency. You must understand, Sebastian, that the brain reacts to the minutest electrical impulse. The power needed to control all the specimens in this room is no greater than that needed to illuminate a pen light bulb."

I was duly impressed, and said so. Then I

130

asked what could be the practical application of such control.

"Come, come, Mr. Cant, use your imagination. A single nurse could control an entire ward of a mental hospital. One prison guard could render hundreds of inmates immobile with the turn of a dial, stopping a riot as easily as turning on a radio."

"Rather than render them immobile, wouldn't it be as easy and more humane to keep them tranquilized by constant stimulation of the pleasure centers?"

"No. One would think so, of course, but we discovered through hard lessons what we should have figured out by simple logic."

"And what is that, Doctor?"

"That pleasure is a relative thing, like all other feelings. You have heard of the idiot who pounds his head against the wall because it feels so good when he stops?" I resisted sarcasm in favor of a simple nod. "It's purely a matter of habituation. If one is adapted to severe pain, then the absence of it evokes a feeling of extreme pleasure, but the absence of that feeling, the discontinuance of it, is painful. Kong, over here, is a good example of this kind of adaptation." Kong was the gorilla. "Beautiful, isn't he?"

"I have a feeling, Doctor, that your boy Kong, here, is not as malevolent as he appears."

131

"True, but he wasn't when we got him, and that is one of the reasons for his acquisition. Kong, it seems, had a sadistic trainer during his upbringing. He was raised in a circus, and the objective of his trainer was apparently to make Kong as vicious as possible to elicit squeals of fear from ladies and children who came near his cage. Whatever his methods . . . torture, deprivation, restraint, or a combination of all three . . . the trainer succeeded beyond his expectation. One day Kong reached out, grabbed the trainer, pulled him to the bars, and twisted his head off. He was to be put to death when we intervened and persuaded the circus to sell him to us for research."

"Us? That's something I wondered about, Doctor. How do you represent yourself to the outside world? You obviously have to purchase food and supplies for Sunnyview. Do you ship everything here yourselves, and if so, do you order and pay for things as Sunnyview Hospital? Or do you have fronts? Dummy companies?" He fidgeted. He did not like the line of questioning at all.

"For the moment, Sebastian, I prefer not to answer those questions. Suffice it to say we have means and methods of getting what we need without disclosing our location. Now, if I may go on . . ." I held out my hand, palm up, indicating the floor was his. He continued:

"Kong had, in that one furious moment, become a man-killer. When he arrived at Sunnyview, he nearly escaped from the first cage we put him in by tearing off the padlock. He was stunned into submission by a tranquilizing gun, but not before he had badly mauled a male nurse. When we secured him in a new, stronger cage, he shook it violently without respite for a week until he simply tired of the exercise. After a term of observation, we operated and implanted the metallic flakes that we call BSCs. They are injected into the brain tissue by hypodermic, after location of the pleasure center by means of electronic probing. The operation was a total success. He responded to stimulation by becoming immediately as docile as a lamb. He loved it. We put him on continued stimulation for several weeks. However, when we turned off the stimulation, he not only reverted to his former aggressive behavior, but it was intensified tenfold. It was then he acquired the name Kong."

"What was his name before?"

"What a curious question. After all I told you, what intrigues you is his former name. Names do obsess you, don't they, Sebastian?"

"What was it? Or is that a secret, Doctor?"

"His name was, if I am not mistaken, Elwood."

"Elwood? Beautiful." I laughed, and looking

at the steel eyes of the beast, I wondered aloud: "What if, Doctor, what if, instead of brain-stimulated pleasure, he had been given love?"

"Love? Don't be childish, Sebastian. The animal tore the head off his trainer. I told you, he is a man-killer."

"One man, Doctor, and by your own description, a sadist who tortured him."

"You fail to see, Sebastian, that our objective was to accomplish absolute foolproof physical control of hostility by means of surgical implantation. That was the sole purpose of our bringing the ape here in the first place. Were he not a vicious animal, implantation would have been a pointless exercise. Admittedly, there is documented evidence that loving care can indeed turn a vicious animal into a docile one *sometimes*. *Our* method always works. It's infallible."

I stared around the room at all those poor inanimate creatures whose natural state was so far removed from the voiceless statues I saw, and I wondered about the hospital inmates and the prisoners Bananastein would have controlled.

"Shall we go to lunch, Sebastian?"

I looked around the room, and then at him questioningly.

"Oh. No, don't worry, I'm not going to leave them fixed."

He held up the little transmittter and turned a dial. There was an immediate perceptible cessation of tension in the room. I glanced at the eyes of Kong, or rather Elwood. The rage in them disappeared as suddenly as a candle going out.

"Now watch," he said, "I will free them to move." He turned another dial. There was immediate vocalizing. The monkeys, baboons, chimps, and Elwood, all were rocking and making little sounds of pleasure. The big gorilla sat back on his haunches and made what can only be described as purring sounds. Bananastein held the face of the transmitter toward me and pointed to the center dial.

"This one controls the pleasure stimulator, Sebastian. Turn it all the way to the left, counter clockwise until it clicks off."

I looked around and settled my gaze on Elwood. This, I thought, is how he looked before the sadistic trainer, before Sunnyview, before man.

"What if I just turned it halfway around, Doctor, not completely off?"

"Try it."

I reached out tentatively and turned the center knob slowly to the left. The effect was nothing less than hysterical. Every chimp in the room looked and acted as if he were drunk. They jabbered and screeched and laughed (it seemed) and staggered around in their cages. Elwood fell over, got up, stood on his head, or tried to, fell over again, and curled up his lips in a monstrous grin. The total effect was funny as hell, and I laughed, to which they all reacted by jumping up and down and falling over, chattering away.

Dr. Bananastein turned the knob up full again and they were at once back in their stupor.

"You can see," he said dryly, "that either full stimulation or none at all is necessary for definitive responses. Setting the knob midway transmits only an infinitesimal charge, resulting in a state of mild inebriation, useless to research." I decided then and there that Bananastein was a champion bore.

"Would you please stand over by the door, Sebastian?"

"What's up next?"

"Next, we leave; but first I must turn off the stimulator, and the reaction from the animals can be frightening even to the initiated."

"Go ahead," I said bravely.

"Suit yourself."

The room was very quiet, save for a few contented soft grumbles here and there. There was a quick low-keyed ratchet sound as Bananas twisted the dial to zero in one snapped turn. What happened next was terrifying. The air was at once filled with fear-filled screeching from every creature in the room except the two of us, and I wasn't sure about me. The screeches were at a scream level, with monkeys large and small banging about their cages, pounding the metal floors and ceilings furiously.

Kong (and he was now indeed Kong) had hold of the bars at the front of his cage, and was throwing his weight back and forth with such raging power that the front and back of the enormously heavy cage alternately lifted and banged down again on the cement floor, sending dust and cement chips flying. His beady eyes were electric with hate.

In a defensive reflex, my hands flew to my ears to try to block out the awful bedlam. A glance around the room revealed that every hate-filled eye was beamed on us. Somehow they knew we had stopped the feeling that they had grown adapted to, and if they were not confined, I am sure they would have torn us to pieces.

With my hands cupped tightly to my ears, I ran for the door. I twisted the knob, the door opened, and I glanced back to the doctor. He was coolly closing the glass case where he had replaced the transmitter, and he turned for one look around the room before he started toward me. Unbelievably, the insane bastard was smiling.

Outside, Bananastein locked the metal-plated door while I stood beside him. I could still hear the muffled din after the door was sealed shut.

"How long will they be in that state?"

"In a few hours they'll settle down to resigned whimpering. What did you think of the demonstration?"

"A bit cruel, isn't it?"

"Try to think of the eventual good that will be accomplished, Sebastian. Think of the elimination of straitjackets in the violent wards of the hospitals. Think of the absolute security of prisons."

"I'm thinking, Doctor, I'm thinking."

We headed back up the long hallway. The ringing in my ears abated and was replaced by our heel clicks on the cold floor. The poor little bastards, I kept thinking; the poor little bastards.

"How about lunch, Sebastian?" he asked cheerily. "I'm hungry."

Dr. Bananastein ate heartily. Perhaps cruelty is exhilarating to the sadist appetite. I hadn't the stomach, literally, for anything heavier than the All-American Martini luncheon. He gorged on steak while I sipped, and between bits he told me of his personal background.

Years ago, he said, he became fascinated with the possibility of eliminating man's

destructive drives by means of physically altering the brain. He and a few close colleagues
agreed that that was the direction their diverse
but parallel research was taking. More and
more, over the years, this small group began to
think of themselves as the vanguard force that
would eventually free man from his worst enemy—his own aggressiveness. Bananas's eyes
glowed as he described the group's solidifica-
tion into one unit, one team, with a common
goal. "A holy crusade," he said. Holy indeed, I
thought.

He told of how he and his cohorts accelerated their progress by sharing the results of
their work, some of which overlapped and
some, to their delight, that dove-tailed beauti-
fully. As they progressed, their number grew
. . . carefully, selectively, but steadily. Bananastein, who had been their sometime leader,
took over fully when he fathered the final
ingredient to complete their revolutionary
treatment, the anti-protein he christened
Oedipium.

The group experimented on animals for
several years, champing at the bit to ply their
new found skills on a *Homo sapiens* or two. After haunting prison wardens and mental hospital directors for a considerable time, unto them
at last was delivered the mind and soul of one
Charles L., killer of children, boiler of sin
bubbles.

Their difficulty in obtaining a human specimen was due largely to the fact that they
would not reveal any detail other than that
they had a foolproof cure for anti-social behavior. They were only able to procure Charley-
boy because of a number of agreed-to con-
tingencies, and the fact that the child-cooker's
attorney had somehow failed to convince a jury
of his client's insanity and Charles was sent to
prison. He, therefore, was considered
competent to volunteer for medical experimentation.

Bananas's raiders agreed to return Charles L.
to prison immediately after treatment, where
he would remain to serve out his sentence. He
would, however, be closely observed with an
eye toward a possible parole hearing if the ex-
perimental treatment proved successful. It was
a total success, and the once-homicidal maniac
was released into the loving arms of civilized
society two years later. Incredibly, the prison
officials were so nervous about possible adverse
publicity they never inquired into the details of
the treatment, allowing Bananastein and his
boys to secure the guinea pig while keeping the
experiment entirely under wraps. No one outside their exclusive clique knew of the achieve-
ment.

Slowly, over the years, they widened their
circle of the members in an interesting way.

They allowed their medical colleagues to know of their results, without revealing their methods. Members of their profession were at first irritated by this exclusory attitude, but overlooked it in the face of their incredible results, and with cautious selectivity even the inner circle was allowed to expand.

The most prolific gain in membership to the extraordinary club was from the ranks of psychiatrists.

In the beginning, word of mouth traveled slowly, always within the medical brotherhood, and psychiatrists would send only their incurable cases to Bananastein and company. But, as the success rate held at nearly 100 percent, the shrinks who were admitted to the club grew at an accelerated rate. More and more, "The Treatment" was considered as a first resort rather than a last. The results were inevitable. The backlog grew to intolerable proportions, and sooner or later the secret treatment would have become public knowledge . . . a possibility Bananastein and his cabal refused to accept.

They resolved their excess demand situation in a tried and true capitalistic manner—they raised their fees. In fact, Bananas said, they raised them to a level out of reach of all but the very wealthy and thus cut down their demand while, with the same stroke, they set up a market that would build an enormous treasury, a fund that would be used to build secluded facilities to house patients and train personnel in their methods. Hence the birth of Sunnyview and ten sister hospitals, each remote and unknown to all but the limited chosen.

I finished off my third martini as Bananastein wiped his chin free of chocolate pudding dessert, and I asked if the secrecy was ever breached, and if not, why?

"No, never," he replied, "and the reason is that we are all, every doctor, every nurse, every member of our staff down to the janitors, totally and absoultely dedicated to a cause greater than ourselves." He placed his napkin alongside his plate.

"Shall we go?" he suggested as he slid back his chair.

"Back to your office?"

"No, I don't think so, Sebastian." He came around to my side of the table.

"I think," he said, "that you have had enough to digest today. Why don't you relax the rest of the afternoon, and I'll see you again tomorrow morning?"

"Will you tell me what I had to forget to get well? Will you tell me all, tomorrow?"

"All, Sebastian, all. We want you back in the fold."

"*Back*?" I echoed. He didn't reply.

"Tomorrow, Sebastian."

"Tomorrow," I agreed, and he was gone. I ordered another refill. I wanted to kill some more time, enough to take me up to five o'clock. I wanted to be in the golf course restaurant at 5:25, and as of that moment I still could not recall exactly why.

10.

FOR the hour that I sat at the table after Dr. Bananastein left, I chewed and rechewed all I had been told that afternoon. The fact is that all sounded somehow right. I didn't like Bananastein, but that was a personal thing. After all, so my reasoning went, if the ends were righteous, perhaps they *did* justify the means. A world without aggression; that was not an evil goal.

Bananastein had said at one point that they were now in the process of constructing a hospital in Europe and one in South America. They already had one in Canada, and their membership—that is, those in the profession who agreed with them and assisted in providing patients—now included nearly one out of every seven psychiatrists in the world. He also strongly hinted that some powerful but sympathetic politicians and philanthropists were within their holy circle.

Perhaps, I thought, this is indeed the answer. Just prior to attacking his chocolate pudding, Bananastein told the story of an Air Force colonel who had undergone treatment. It seemed that this colonel, who was a confirmed bachelor until his fortieth year, got married and promptly slipped his clutch. He held a potentially dangerous position of authority in the upper echelons of the Strategic Air Command. One busy day in the war room of a SAC command base at the height of a simulated attack maneuver, he leaped to his feet and declared at the top of his lungs that San Francisco was a more deserving target than Moscow. Homosexuality, not communism, was the more dangerous enemy, he railed, and was escorted from the room by military police.

After examination by flight surgeon psychiatrists, hospitalization was prescribed. Somewhere along in his treatment, a doctor had the anti-fruit colonel shipped surreptitiously to a Sunnyview.

In relatively short order, the colonel was released back through Air Force channels to resume his delicate job, devoid of any urges to drop nuclear weapons on Finnochio's.

How does one fault a case result like that, I argued. Still, through all my rational thinking, there pervaded a feeling that something was not quite right. What does one do if, after long cool appraisal, the blocks of logic fit together with geometric perfection and one still hears a whimpering, primitive voice deep in the soul wailing without reason: "It is wrong; it is wrong."

These thoughts occupied my mind until late afternoon when I made my way to the nineteenth hole restaurant.

I seated myself at the same table that I had occupied the night before. I peered through the same window, searching the outer edges of Sunnyview's grounds, waiting for the appearance of whatever it was that disturbed me the night before. It was five o'clock.

I ordered a light salad and a cut of medium-rare steak, determined to get enough food in me to slow the effect of the martinis, but not heavy enough to encourage drowsiness.

As the hands moved toward the anticipated time, I scanned the golf course and my attention was attracted to a reflective metallic glinting along a wide path running parallel to the line between Sunnyview's open grounds and the surrounding woods. My suspicions demanded closer inspection, for if it was what I thought it was, then everything was at once changed. All bets were off, as the expression goes.

As I finished off my steak, I took care to note landmarks, as one does to pinpoint the landing spot of an off-the-midway golf shot before leaving the tee. My objective lay conveniently between twin pines about twenty feet in height and roughly thirty yards in from the termination of the grass and the start of the woods. It was a short, quick walk from the restaurant, and as I approached my destination I slowed to an affected aimless meandering. After several pieces of hamming and whistling, I sidled to the edge of the woods. Satisfied no eye was on me, I ambled toward the shrubbery that glittered so unnaturally. Once upon it, I could see the cause of the reflections. The leaves were spotted with tiny metal flakes, of the size and type that are sprayed on cheap stucco homes.

Being careful not to touch, I bent over to more closely examine, and I heard over my shoulder the unmistakable fluttering blades and engine sound of an approaching helicopter. In a moment it was overhead, but not before I vainly fell into my ambling, rambling act. A loudspeaker crackled out my name.

"Mr. Cant, please report to the main building. Mr. Cant, please report to the main building."

I obeyed and headed for Bananastein's white castle, secure in the knowledge that I had discovered what Frost's "something" doesn't love; electronic, ultra-modern, cunning and unique; but by any other name . . . a wall. I held tight reins on the panic that surged in my chest. I knew if I even turned my head away from the main building and toward the woods I would give way, and in an instant be running in blind fear for freedom. I held tight, and with draining force kept my control until I reached the entrance to the main building where Banana-stein stood waiting. I followed him dumbly down the corridor and into his office. He proceeded directly to his damnable bar, and I took up a position with my back to the closed office door. I was trembling.

"I sent for you, Sebastian, because there are a few more things I thought we should ..."

"There's no need for that."

"What do you mean?" he said, pouring a drink and avoiding my eyes.

"I know it's a fence. I know that swath of metal flaking running the edge of the woods is an electronic fence. All this time, I've been a prisoner, haven't I, Doctor?"

"Prisoner is a harsh word, Sebastian."

"Come off it, Doctor, that cliché is usually used when one is accused of blackmail. Harsh or not harsh, there is no other word. I'm a prisoner."

"It is necessary, once treatment has commenced, to assure that the patient remains until he is cured."

"Cured? What the hell are you talking about? You've explained to me the method of treatment. The hallucinations, the nightmares, that was all part of it. I accept that. But for the past week you have been engaged in sales-pitching me to stay on. That is not part of your bloody treatment. Your tinsel-leaved fence is designed to restrict and contain *everyone* at Sunnyview. Period. My treatment is over, and cured or not, I can't leave. The rest is bullshit."

"You must know everything before you decide, Sebastian!" He slammed the butt of his fist down hard on the bar nearly spilling his drink. I could hear the heel-clicks again. Hitler was back.

"I know everything . . ." I trailed off. I gave up the argument before I began. What was the point? I wanted away from Sunnyview and I wasn't going to talk my way out. I'd have to escape.

"We ended our conversation this afternoon on an unanswered question, Mr. Cant." He freshened his drink with more ice and soda. It was a senseless action, since he had not even tasted it, but the point of it was to display his regained cool.

"Which was?"

"Which was, why I used the expression 'back in the fold,' implying you were here before." The son-of-a-bitch had me hooked again.

"Okay, why did you? Was I at Sunnyview before?"

"No. No, you were never here before this

visit, Sebastian, but you were in the fold; that is, you were one of us."

"A doctor?" The idea was staggering. Had they erased from my brain years of medical education and practice? Years of living, of being a doctor, leaving not a trace? I grew suddenly very angry at the possibility and it must have showed.

"Put your mind at ease, Sebastian, you were never a doctor."

He held up an empty glass. "Will you join me?"

"Thanks. I'll have a weak one. Bourbon and ginger."

"I don't think it will greet that gin and vermouth too pleasantly. How about a martini?"

"Whatever."

He drew out of the bar fridge one of those half-pint cocktail bottles unscrewed the cap, and poured.

"All right, Doctor, what was I, then? What was my job in the holy inner circle?" He glanced disapprovingly at my sarcastic tone.

"Do you remember your connection with us?"

He handed me my drink, sat in his chair, and stirred his drink idly with a green plastic swizzle. He was studying me.

"You don't know, Doctor, do you?"

"Know what?" He shrugged his shoulders

and tapped the swizzle on the rim of his glass before placing it on the coffee table.

"It's plain you are not sure how much I remember about my job and its connection to you and your group. I am beginning to suspect that any treatment I have undergone here was not for the purpose of eradicating guilt over my daughter's death, but rather to eliminate knowledge that represented a danger to you. Information useful as blackmail? Or was it simply that I was going to expose the new and glorious Reich to the world? Was that it? A matter of keeping my mouth shut by the simple expediency of wiping my brain clean. Am I right?"

"Yes and no."

"Goddamn it! I'm not in the mood for any more games!" I was on my feet and mad enough to hit. He realized it and paled.

"If you have any notion of assaulting me, put it out of your head at once. It will gain you nothing and cost you dearly."

I got my nerves controlled but I didn't sit. I was too hot. I took a heavy swallow of my martini and began pacing, collecting my thoughts and arranging what I wanted to say. It struck me that now I was on my feet and Bananastein was seated, waiting to hear what I had to say. The reversal of our roles hit my funnybone, dissipating my anger.

"Will you answer what I ask?" I said, neither threateningly nor pleadingly.

"Yes."

I walked over to the window and threw my first question over my shoulder. "Did I have any real guilt in the death of my daughter, and was it justified?"

"Yes, in answer to both questions."

"Elucidate, please."

"From the beginning? More or less?"

"More or less."

"When you were a child, Sebastian, you had, as near as we can guess, a babysitter, a nurse or governess, who tended you. This nanny, and we know it was she and not your mother, had a mental aberration that was singular and very sick indeed."

"Regarding urination?" I interrupted.

"Yes."

"How is it that I know that? How can I be cured and still recall . . ."

"The nightmares? The hallucinations?"

"Yes."

"You realize that the hallucinations and nightmares regarding urination were induced here at Sunnyview, and were not real, don't you, Sebastian?"

"Yes."

"To further assure you, I am telling you here and now, if you haven't guessed already, that they were manifestations of your long-held repressed remembrances of the experiences with your nanny as a child, brought to the surface as a necessary part of your treatment."

"Brought to the surface to be erased."

"Exactly, Sebastian."

"Some baby tender. I wonder where my parents got her?"

"Does it matter? If she is alive today, she may still be practicing her strange habit, and no doubt it sprang from some trauma *she* experienced. But that is what we are all about, my young friend. Curing sickness by the most effective means yet devised by medical science. Are we so evil?"

I avoided response to the question. "Please go on, Doctor." I sat down and sipped at the last of my drink.

"There are some mental illnesses that present themselves in overt symptoms that are observable and therefore detectable. There are others that are resolved by the afflicted by secretive means and are never detected. Some of these types are not even what we would truly classify as mentally ill, such as transvestites or closet homosexuals, but there are others whose illness is very real . . . sadists, rapists, or child molesters. There are those such as child beaters and the likes of your baby tender, as you call her, whose unwilling victims are infants who cannot publicize. These people can do horrible damage and never be uncovered."

"Except, perhaps, by your methods, thank God." I actually said that. There I sat, rah-rahing for old Sunnyview U. The good doctor smiled benignly in righteous gratitude.

"We do what we can," he said bravely.

"Now you said, Doctor, you concerned yourself primarily with aggressive anti-social behavior. Did my repressed trauma express itself in such behavior before the incident of my daughter's death?" It surprised me that I could speak of little Annie so objectively.

"Yes. We discussed in my office, you recall, the experience in the restaurant with your sister? Where you threw your graduation gift in her face?"

"Yes, I remember. A watch . . . right?"

"That's correct. There were numerous other . . ."

"Excuse me, Doctor. I'm sorry to interrupt, but would you digress for a moment and tell me about my daughter's death? Would you tell me exactly what happened? Accidentally or not, did I actually push her out a window?"

"I will tell you all about that, Sebastian, but in the proper sequence, please."

"Oh, damn the continuity! I want to hear about my daughter. What difference will it make in what order you relate the events?"

"It does, Sebastian. Please exercise half as

154

much patience with me as I am exercising with you."

"Well, patience is easy, Doctor, for a prisoner. It comes with the sentence, doesn't it?"

He was on his feet.

"I'll tell you flatly, Sebastian, there are those who hold to the opinion that I have gone overboard in my patience with you. I answer them that you are worth the effort, but I am fast losing that argument, even with myself."

"What do those others suggest, Doctor? That you do away with me?"

"Something like that, *Mr.* Cant! Something like that!"

"My, my. I believe that is what is called your standard, straight-out threat."

"I tire of this banter, Sebastian. It is nonproductive, to say the least. You were caught out there in what was an obvious attempt to leave Sunnyview without notice or authority."

"If I gave notice, and I would assume thirty days is customary, would I get the authority? And why do you studiously avoid the ever-popular and honest verb *escape*?"

"You will do very well, Sebastian . . . and I advise this benevolently . . . to listen to everything I have to tell you and not set yourself rashly in an irreversible direction. The hour draws late."

I studied his eyes carefully. There was no

155

doubt that this was an ultimatum and I should give it no less consideration. I decided again, this time I hoped with stronger resolve, to keep my fool mouth shut until I was ready to go one way or the other and it looked like a fish-or-cut-bait choice was not far off. I nodded in submission and he continued.

"Along with the incident with your sister, there were numerous other outbursts of violence in your youth, most of which you got by with. That is, you did not hurt anyone badly enough to interest the police or school authorities, etcetera. When you were eighteen, you joined the service and were shipped to Vietnam, and not a moment too soon, I might add."

"Oh?"

"Yes. Like so many others who are prone to anti-social violence, war was the ideal setting for release. There you were not only allowed to give full vent to your repressed rages, but for doing so, you were rewarded. You came out of that conflict with a chest full of medals. And went to work for the West Coast Stock Exchange. In three industrious years you had become a broker. When you reached a level where your accounts were pretty much controlled by you autonomously, we approached you."

"If I'm not interrupting, why me?"

"Well, for one thing, you needed money. You went heavily into debt when you tried to recoup a small loss and gambled in a very chancy stock acquisition. But more important, you needed medical help. You had developed an ulcer, and were seeing a psychiatrist; a doctor with whom we had more than a nodding acquaintance. He knew of our need for front companies to shield our organization from public scrutiny, and he saw in you, and rightly so, a golden opportunity for a mutually agreeable alliance."

"That's a long way round to say you had me by the balls."

"Not true. You needed us, Sebastian, more than we needed you. You developed an ulcer, but that was a mild manifestation of your illness. You were, to be exact, ready and primed for violent expression again, and you somehow sensed that it might lead to something very bad, even murder.

"We reached an agreement with you. We would embark on a full-scale treatment if you would set up two dummy corporations for us, but you wanted more. You wanted us to wipe out all your debts. We agreed. Your psychiatrist kept you under control with tranquilizers while you took care of the necessary business to establish two companies that would serve our needs, but then disaster struck in the form of your daughter's accident, just as you completed your work.

"Your daughter was visiting you at your apartment. Her name was Annie. She was seven years old and was one of two offspring of a mismatched contract that lasted less than three years. The day of the accident was one of her scheduled visitation days under the terms of the custody agreement reached by you and your former wife. Your son did not come with his sister. He had the flu, and stayed in bed.

"You brilliantly decided that you didn't want to be drugged, as you put it, when you saw her, so you elected to dispense with your prescribed dose of tranquilizers that day. When, during the course of the visit, the child began discussing her mother, you railed at her with such fury she wet her pants. This purely innocent and, under the circumstances, natural reaction touched that deep, tender spot in your psyche, and your anger turned into unbridled rage. You apparently did not touch her, but rather vented your fury on the furniture, breaking and smashing everything in sight. The child, now utterly terrified, ran to the open window and leaned out screaming for help. A neighbor directly across the air shaft, which was no more than thirty feet wide, testified that the child was apparently without injury, merely frightened. This neighbor could plainly see you in the background breaking something or other. The child leaned too far and . . ." He stopped because I was crying. "I'm sorry, Sebastian." He went to the bar where he fetched a box of Kleenex. "Here."

"Thank you."

"Do you want me to continue, or would you rather some other time?"

"No. Go on. I want to hear all of it."

"During the inquest, you unfortunately elected to tell all about our organization, about the drugs you were taking, about our agreements, etcetera. Had these revelations been delivered from the witness box in a cool, controlled manner, the judge might have given them some credibility, but, fortunately for all concerned, you chose to rant and rave at the top of your lungs. All that was needed was testimony by your psychiatrist, whose loyalties were of course with us. He testified under oath that you were a psychotic suffering from extreme paranoia. You pleaded that you could produce documented proof of fraud. In short, Sebastian, you were, in your deranged fury, bent on destroying us, and, of course, we could not allow that."

"So you got me to Sunnyview and proceeded to erase from my memory all that was potentially dangerous to you."

"That is correct," he said without apology.

"What about this associative reaction baloney, about the crazy governess I had, and my need to do violence?"

"She was very real, but all of that has been taken care of, Sebastian; you are a well man now, cured of that problem entirely. It will not reoccur."

"Tell me, Doctor, I must have realized that I didn't kill my daughter at the time. I mean, if I was busy breaking furniture, as you say the neighbor testified, I must have known that I did not actually push her. I must have known that it was an accident."

"You did."

"Then tell me this; could I not have been cured without my entire childhood obliterated from my mind?"

"We haven't erased your entire childhood."

"What the hell do you mean? I can't remember any of it, so I should be the best judge of that. And what about the other big gaps . . . my marriage . . . my time in the service . . . in school? Was it necessary to take all of that?"

"Some of it, yes. Some, no. Some of it went with the current, as it were."

"With the current? What does that mean?"

"Well, this treatment is not all that precise, Sebastian. We are not dealing with a tape recorder, we are dealing with a human brain. If you brought out of your memory experiences we were not concerned with at the same time that you brought to the surface those of import, we could not separate them. Memories are often intertwined, enmeshed, and overlapping. We cannot separate them. We are not that far advanced."

"So when you spotted something that had to go, it all went. Is that it? You just washed out whole sections, years of my life, right?"

"You are still the same man you were, Sebastian, minus the propensity for anti-social violence."

"Then tell me something, Doctor, why do I have an overwhelming urge to kill you?"

"The fact that you are not doing precisely that is proof that the urge is not overwhelming but, in fact, controllable."

I didn't know what I was like before my visit to Sunnyview, but I was raging inside at the moment and would have, I'm sure, felt exquisite satisfaction in watching his eyeballs bug out from the force of my hands around his throat. But he was right: I controlled; I maintained.

"Can you tell me something else, Doctor?"

"Go ahead."

"If you hadn't needed me for your nefarious stock dealings and if I hadn't threatened to blow the whistle, would I still have been a candidate for your treatment? Would I still have wound up at Sunnyview with half my life's memories pulled from my mind and destroyed?"

"That, my dear Sebastian, is a moot point on a *fait accompli*. A useless argument that will serve no purpose. Am I right?"

I could say nothing. I did not have Bananastein's faith in my self-control, and I felt sure that whatever words started from my mouth would crescendo into a primal scream, and I would be on him, not to be torn free before I stopped his breathing. He said something about it being time for supper and asked if I would return early the next day to his office. I held myself together somehow, told him I would, and left the office.

I headed for the cafeteria, not for sustenance, but to collar John Macky. Between my exit from the main building and my entrance into the dorm, I had convinced myself of two things: escape alone was impossible, and the saint wanted to leave. How I came to the latter conclusion I can't explain except to say it was intuitive.

When I spotted John, I didn't ask for his time, I simply grabbed an elbow, and with furtive gestures, hustled him up to my room, where he collapsed in a chair, agape at my pronouncement.

"I'm going over the hill, John."

"Now look," he said, "I don't know what brought this on, Sebastian, but you know that you can leave Sunnyview anytime..."

"Don't do that, Saint."

"Do what? What are you talking...?"

"Don't bullshit me, Saint. I mean, I don't think I could take that. I'm feeling very nervous." I was shaking with such hot intensity I could have toasted bread between my hands.

"I saw that bloody electronic doohickey fence, John, so please, *please*, don't try to blow any smoke up my tush. Just tell me two things: can I make it out of here, and will you go with me?"

He answered and, as he did, his facial expression subtly belied everything he said. His voice said, calmly and soothingly, that I was imagining things, that I didn't really mean escape, since in spite of what I might have seen I could truly leave any time I wished to go, etc., etc., but as he said these things in even unstrained tones, his eyes burned and darted from side to side in a manner that indicated he was either purposefully denouncing what he was saying, or he was a madman.

I fell into his act with him, slowly allowing myself to be calmed and quieted. It was clear that either John knew the room was bugged, or strongly suspected it. I had to be careful not to change my demeanor too abruptly, lest whoever had his ear to the drinking glass tip to my ruse. Sunnyview was producing a first-rate actor, I thought.

In due course, after some brilliant histrionics, during which I crashed a lamp to the floor for effect, I allowed John Macky to talk me into a drink in the Winter room, and we proceeded downstairs.

The rest of that evening we carried on the strangest conversation I had ever engaged in. We talked about Julie, who, John explained, had been once again assigned to swing-shift duty. He assured me that it was not a ploy to keep us apart, but the necessary and normal staggering of schedules. We talked about golf and made plans for a game early the next morning. John assured me that Bananas never sees patients before 9 or 10 A.M., and that we would thus have time for a relaxed nine holes if we started early.

Whenever there were lapses in the conversation, John would stare hard into my eyes, sending to me with urgent clarity the messages that we were being overheard, or watched, or both. He was speaking to me in a language that must have been practiced by our ancient forebears long before onomatopoetic grunting, and I understood.

We burned away the balance of the evening's candle this way, until an appropriate hour for retirement, and later, as I trudged the dimly lit stairwell and hallway to my room, I speculated on a variety of questions regarding Saint John Macky. How, and under what circumstances, did he discover he was being surveilled? Had he, himself, ever tried to escape? Or was he waiting, hoping, for an ally to effect some long-ago-formulated perfect plan that required more than one escapee for faultless execution?

Or, lastly, and most depressingly, had I incorrectly interpreted Macky's furtive eyeball-rolling and hard, significant stares to be secret communications, and were they, in reality, merely paranoidal signs of a man overcooked in that fruitcake bakery?

I undressed, letting my clothes fall in a wrinkling pile, and crawled into bed, cozying myself with thoughts of Julie.

"Arnie, Arnie, wake up!" Some fool, using my one shoulder for a pivot, was rocking me on the bed by the other.

"Leggo, leggo. Sleep. Go away. I wanna sleep. Leggo."

"Arnie, please! Mr. Palmer, your fans are waiting!" I ceased muscular resistance and Saint John rolled me onto my back.

"What the hell do you want?" I squinted up at him, the ceiling light hurting my eyes.

"Time to rise, if not shine, good buddy. Sunnyview's answer to Pebble Beach awaits."

"Oh, yeah, yeah. What time is it, John? Turn off that light, will you?"

"Why? You'll get used to it. Come on," he urged. "It's after five A.M. already."

"Bastard."

"*Tch, tch, tch.* Very hostile. Very hostile indeed. Must be a fierce-type person. Come on, come on, soldier, on your feet." He had placed his tennis-shoed foot on the edge of the mattress and was pumping the bed into a violent rocking motion.

"Okay, okay. Get your goddamn foot off my bed, tramp!" I forced my legs off the mattress and onto the floor and sat up with my head in my hands.

"What time is it?"

"You already asked me that, Arnie."

I rubbed my eyes and scratched my head. "Five? Is it really five?"

"After five."

I didn't look up but just sat there with my elbows on my bony knees, rubbing my face with the flats of my hands.

"Did anyone ever tell you, Mr. Palmer, that you are truly beautiful in the morning?"

I rose to my feet, prodded by both the saint's shrewish insistence and an urgent bladder. In short order, I had taken care of, as they say in the service, the three S's, and I was ready. We made it to the cafeteria, where we sat among the empty chairs and tables, sipping hot, hot coffee. We were alone, save for two bedraggled nurses, each off by herself and wearing the tired look of a hard day's night.

John paused between slurps to give me that fixed look again that warned me to keep the chatter safely insignificant. I nodded as imperceptibly as I could and was feeling for all the world like an espionage agent in a foreign restaurant. We fell to exchanging golf jokes, the saint easily outdoing me. It struck me so odd that we should be laughing when the situation was so grave and our plans so perilous.

"More coffee?" John was on his feet, holding our two cups, awaiting my reply. His annoyed tone indicated this was not the first time he asked.

"Oh, I'm sorry, Saint. Yes, please."

I watched him as he refilled our cups from a large urn at the end of the tray-slide chow line. The cooks were setting up rectangular metal basins of food, gently fitting them into matching apertures in the steam table. I was reminded at once of the Army chow halls. The rough talk and tattoos were missing, but the white-hatted cooks still had that same hustle in their movements, and the general ambience was all there. I thought of the times I was on KP, and it pained me suddenly to realize that I could not remember the glorious days of battle that Bananastein talked about, but I could, however, remember my time served as a potato skinner.

John came back, holding each mug out and away from his body to allow for slop. He placed mine before me and snapped his hand free of hot spill.

"Going to see Bananastein today?" His abrupt reference to the doctor, and by that moniker, threw me for an instant. Were we now suddenly out of monitoring range and able to talk freely? But a quick knitting of John's eyebrows and a second's reflection told me that we were not, and that John was only trying to sound convincingly unaware to any would-be listener. I picked up my coffee and sipped it, as if that were the reason for my hesitation.

"Hot stuff," I commented.

"Yes."

"I go to see the old fart this morning about nine-ish. You know, John, some of the things he's been telling me make good sense . . . I mean, he's not quite the ogre I originally thought he was. In fact, the old boy's got a keen sense of humor." I said that. I really did.

"He's okay," agreed John, "but he's too dogmatic for me. Too stiff-lipped." John, the better actor, was tempering my accolades with a dash of criticism, aware that bullshit has a detectable aroma.

"Yes, I suppose." The strain of this charade was getting to me, and I was anxious to get someplace where we could speak freely.

"About time to hit the links, John?"

"Right on, Mr. Palmer. Ready any time you are."

I gulped down the rest of my coffee in three hot swallows as I stood up and started for the door.

"You can leave the cup here, Seb."

I'll be damned, I thought, as I placed the cup on the table. This place really does remind me of a service mess hall. I was all set to carry my cup to an imaginary dish rack near the exit. I could see myself pushing upon the springloaded exit doors, reaching to my rear pocket for my fatigue cap, and strutting down a dirt path in some nearly forgotten Army base.

Away from the dorm by a hundred yards, I was sure it was safe to talk and I could no longer contain myself. "Can we ... ?"

"Oh, sure," John quickly interrupted, "sure, we can get on all right. This time of morning we'll almost have the course to ourselves." His eyes fixed mine for a second, again with that barely perceptible stern expression that flashed a caution light.

Where in the world could there be a bug, I wondered. Is it possible that they could pick up conversation out of the air? No matter, I thought; better to guess on the side of caution. We walked in silence until we reached the clubhouse entrance. Suddenly the saint grabbed the lower front of my jacket and lifted it high above my belt line.

"Well, well, the chow really agrees with you, Seb." He patted my belly in obvious reference to my expanding gut.

"Got to watch that, fella," he said cheerily as we stepped inside the doors of the clubhouse. He had relaxed suddenly. Could it be we were out of danger of surveillance inside the clubhouse? No, that made no sense. Then it struck me that the saint had just given me a light frisk. He thought I was wired, or at least suspected that I might be. Well, I'll be damned, I thought, and I looked at the boyish, freckled face of John Macky with reappraising eyes. No naive trusting bumpkin he . . . not by a mile.

I selected an aluminum "lazy caddy," one of those lightweight club racks that you stick in the ground, rather than a tiring shoulder bag. I wanted to be ready for any possible dash into the jungle. I was already mentally primed and anxious for such a trot.

We were teeing off the fourth hole and the saint still had said absolutely nothing of significance, so I contained myself and engaged only in trivial banter. I was determined that I would not again breach our security. Too, I began to wonder whether, in this matter, my imagination was not again at work making something out of nothing. After all, my only evidence that the saint was going to conspire with me was some furtive glares that could easily have been misinterpreted.

But after we had teed off and were strolling down the fairway, the saint put out his arm to stop me and pointed to the edge of the woods about thirty yards to our right. There, sitting up on his haunches, ears erect, scanning, was a large cottontail. He lowered to his forelegs, took a few short quick hops toward us onto the grass apron, and stood up again. John lowered his golf bag from his shoulder to the ground, and glanced at me as if to say "watch this." He held his cupped hands about a foot apart, then suddenly brought them together with a sharp loud clap. Peter Big-Ears was off with the crack in a long backward hop from dead still; then with three zigzag bounds he disappeared into his woods. Saint John looked at me, then up, and scanned the sky all around to our left, then all around to our right, and to make sure I got the message, he repeated the ritual . . . and I understood. *There were no helicopters.* The rabbit had not triggered the alarm when he traversed the electronic fence!

At the sixth hole John was the first to tee off. I plunked on the bench to await my turn, and the saint inserted a tee in the sod and placed a ball atop it. He then took a couple of customary practice swings after which, instead of standing up to the ball to drive, he approached me.

"Do you have a P pill, Seb? I have a headache." I reached for my kit at my belt but it wasn't there.

"I'm sorry, Saint, I left it back at the dorm, I guess."

"So did I," he said, lifting his jacket to expose his belt.

"If you want, Saint, we can call it a morning." I was ready to quit, since it was abundantly apparent that John was keeping his lip buttoned tight, if indeed he had anything to say in the first place.

"Let's go to the nine anyway, Arnie." He approached his teed-up ball, settled into his stance, and swung at a good shot sending the ball a hundred yards up the middle. He stepped back, and with a wave and bow invited me to tee up. Accompanying myself with mock braggadocio I set up, dug in my heels, and cracked the ball a mighty slice into a sandtrap just off the apron.

John laughed in genuine humor, and was even more relaxed than he had been earlier. He slapped my back and commented something about my being out of shape as we trudged up the fairway. Still grinning, he said in a whisper through slightly parted teeth, "Don't talk loud. Keep it low." My heartbeat picked up its pace and my stomach listed slightly.

"I understand," I whispered in reply.

"If you bow your head like this when you talk and keep your voice low they can't pick it up or read your lips." I nodded. He continued bowing his head, whispering, and looking up to chatter golf talk, then looking down again to whisper. I replied in kind, keeping my end of the conversation limited as much as possible to grunts, acknowledging comprehension.

"You saw the rabbit *not* trigger the fence?"

"Uh huh."

"No metal."

"No metal?"

"Yes. Takes metal. A kit, belt buckle, shoe nails, etcetera. No metal, no alarm."

We reached the saint's ball, and he took a stance back away to take a few practice swings. He allowed his voice to rise a bit in volume, apparently feeling securely out of range. He picked up tufts of grass from in front of the ball, scraped at the face of the iron with his thumbnail, and stood back of the ball to line it up with the flag, talking all the while and even allowing time for me to ask a question:

"If you took off your shoes, belt, kit, etcetera, could you get through, Saint?"

"No."

"Why not?"

"Powdered metal interwoven in waistband, seams of uniform."

"Nice."

"Can be removed . . . then cleaned . . . then no problem . . . right through." He swung at last and chipped the ball nicely up on to the green where it rolled to within three feet of the pin.

"Like a rabbit," he added aloud with a wink.

I had totally forgotten my ball to that point, and only remembered when the saint indicated the sandtrap with his putter. I trudged on into the trap where I took the first series of four strokes necessary to get my ball on the green. Still the furthest away from the hole, I hunched over my ball to line up my shot and took the opportunity for a second more significant question.

"Why are you telling me these things, John?"

He half squatted on one heel, opposite me in line with the ball and hole, gesturing as though he were guiding my aim, but his words had nothing to do with golf, nothing at all.

"I want to leave Sunnyview. I think two would stand a better chance of making it all the way."

I dropped in a genuflect behind the ball as if I were lining it up.

"Why do you want to escape, John?"

"Disappointment . . . disillusion. Does it matter?"

"No. Do you have any kind of plan?"

"Yes. You see, what is needed is a diversion . . . something that will set the place rioting, and I have the key to that diversion." He smiled at his secret. "Something that will be more fun than a barrel of monkeys," he said.

I putted and not surprisingly missed by a five-foot overshot.

"Never up, never in," I commented.

"How about tomorrow?" he said aloud and startled me. "Can you go another nine rounds tomorrow, Seb?"

"I'm ready if you are," I said, with all the meaning in the world. He reached out and grabbed my hand and shook it. A natural gesture appropriate to the end of a golf game, or, likewise, to the sealing of a pact.

John picked up his golf bag lying off the apron, and proceeded toward the clubhouse at a brisk pace. I went after my "Lazy Caddy" on the far side of the green. On the way I spotted a lost ball, picked it up, and seeing it was one more than the caddy would hold in its rack, I shoved it in my jacket pocket. When I did so, I felt something in what I thought was the empty pocket. I knew at once what it was.

"Hey, Saint," I yelled. "Wait up!" and I half trotted, half walked until I caught up with him.

"Whoa, buddy, you have long legs."

"Mine aren't too long, Seb, yours are too short." He smiled his yahoo smile.

"Look," I said.

I held out my hand and opened it to show him. "It's my kit. I must have shoved it in my pocket and forgot it. Still want a P pill? Still got that headache?"

His face blanched of color. His lips impossibly seemed to be whiter than the surrounding skin, and he stared at the kit in my open hand as if I held a tarantula. He sank slowly to his knees, letting the golf bag strap slide from his shoulder and the bag itself drop, half dumping out the clubs. He put both his spread hands over his eyes, and his mouth and face grimaced in the shape of a scream, except there was no sound.

That was why he raised my jacket to look at my belt. That was why he asked if I had a P pill. He wanted to be sure I hadn't worn my kit. *The damnable things were transmitters.* As the realization of what I had done hit me fully, the fluttering beast came whirring over the treetops and the speakers blared: "Hold still down there. Hold still, please, we are landing."

It settled, blowing the grass in changing shades like the nap of velours. One white-clad orderly hopped out of the small gyro, and in a crouched dash cleared the blades, then straightening up, ran over to us.

"Mr. Macky, will you come with us? You're wanted at the main building."

Not "you're under arrest." Not an order, but a request. A simple, innocent request, and I wondered as John walked of his own will to the helicopter and got in, whether I'd ever see him again. I also wondered why they didn't take me, and as the helicopter blades kicked into high gear I began to go over in my mind the whispered conspiratorial conversation. Had I really verbally agreed to escape? Or hadn't I merely listened and nodded once in a while? As the copter flattened the grass and rose in the air, I turned and headed for the clubhouse, my insides as cold as stone with fear.

After the helicopter swooped away with the saint, I had walked to the clubhouse, where I turned in my clubs and carrier. I was acting for all the world as if I had just returned from a pleasant round of golf and nothing unusual had happened, when the reality was that the Sunnyview Gestapo had swallowed my partner for a suspected crime. The man who stood behind the counter and received my equipment asked if I had had a good game. "Yes, thank you," I had replied with a smile, as natural as a sane man.

I gave serious consideration to making a mad dash for freedom, but I suppressed the urge. There was no doubt that they were anticipating such a move and would be on me before I had gotten ten yards into the woods. No. The fact that they had not taken me along with Saint John was not an oversight. Either they did not believe that I was actually going to escape or they still thought I could be persuaded to stay . . . still thought they could change my mind. Change my mind. I shuddered at the new meaning of that once-innocent phrase.

My aimless wandering led me to the entrance of the main building. Oh well, I thought, my schedule calls for an interview with the great Bananastein, and as long as I was not going to bound into the woods like a panicked gazelle, I might just as well stick to my itinerary as vary from it.

All along the trek down the hallway, nurses, doctors, orderlies, and patients floated by me like white-clad ghosts, not saying a word nor giving any sign of greeting, as if they all knew I was a traitor.

I reached Bananas's office. I put my hand on the doorknob and took a deep breath, and walked in.

"Good morning, Sebastian. How are you this bright, cheery day?"

"Fine," I answered and just stood there, just inside the door, not knowing exactly what to do or say. It would not have surprised me if he took a gun from his desk and shot me, or if he exploded in a vilifying rage, or if he wept and wailed, emitting groans of disappointment at my character. All of these reactions were considered in the realm of plausibility by my fibrillating heart, but I was totally unprepared for no reaction whatever, and it was all the more frightening.

"Sit down, Sebastian, you look for all the world like you are about to cut and run."

Aha, I thought, it's cat and mouse time. I was about to nip that game in the bud with a blurted confession, when second thoughts persuaded me to hold. What if I was in no danger, or for that matter, not guilty of anything?

Perhaps they interpreted the conversation between John and me differently than I had assumed they would. I tried to go over the dialogue in my mind, but I couldn't concentrate in the circumstance of being in Bananas's office. In any case, I elected to let him take the lead and I would follow warily, volunteering nothing.

"Care for a cigar, Mr. Cant?" He held the opened cedar box.

"Yes, thank you." I took one and sat down. He stretched out a light for me.

"Some people," he said between puffs as he lighted his own cigar, "some people think that . . ." puff . . . "cigars in the . . ." puff . . . "morning are . . ." puff . . . "vulgar." He snapped the lighter shut and pocketed it. "What do you think, Sebastian Cant?"

"Oh, I don't know."

"Why do you want to leave us, Mr. Cant?"

I felt my forehead grow moist.

"I beg your pardon?"

"Oh come, come, Sebastian, you know what you said to John Macky. You know what you both discussed . . . planned while you were innocently playing golf. And what is more important, you know that we know, so let's not engage in pointless fencing."

"Those kits we wear are radio transmitters, aren't they?"

"Yes. But that is irrelevant. You haven't an-

179

swered the question. Why do you want to leave us?"

"Because ..."

"Go on."

"Because I can't leave."

"Oh please, Sebastian, don't give me any of that philosophical bleating about fences. Do you wish to scale a fence and leap to your death from the observation platform of the Empire State Building simply because the barrier has been put there to contain you?"

"It's not the same thing."

"It is the same thing!" His fist crashed to the coffee table with such force that the cigar box jumped clean off the table top, spilling the contents at my feet.

"It is precisely the same thing! Allowing our patients to leave prematurely is allowing them to place themselves in grave jeopardy. Until they are totally prepared, anything at all could disturb them in a profound enough way to bring about severe and perhaps fatal depression. Depression, my dear Sebastian, can kill; its bottom line is suicide."

"John Macky worked here, Doctor. Wasn't he *cured*? Don't tell me he was still a patient, if in fact he ever was one."

"He was. And relapse is not unknown to any cure, Sebastian. John Macky had a severe relapse, aided, if not initiated, by your influence."

It was again clear to me that I was dealing with an obsessive egotist who could not let reality interfere with his reasoning processes. The problem was that I could not hold to that truth long enough to see *all* of what he had to say in that light. The problem was that he had a cunning mind, and his manic side only surfaced in brief moments of rage. Once calmed, he again appeared to be totally rational, and his reasoning was oppressively flawless.

"I know what you are thinking, Sebastian."

"Do you?"

"Yes. You think, Sebastian Cant . . ." He took a long puff and blew a cloud toward the ceiling . . . "you think Bananastein is crazy as a loon. An obsessive mad doctor type. Am I right?"

Incredible. Here he was again being rational. Thoroughly aware of his image as perceived by others; an ability, I always thought, possessed only by the nonneurotic few.

"I *am* obsessive, Sebastian. I am obsessive about what I perceive to be *the* only salvation of the human race; the constructive control of man's basic nature. The human personality is shaped by memory, by experience, which control the shape and substance of the personality. We can turn a Jack the Ripper into a social human being. We can do that and, therefore, having that power, we *must* use it."

"Is that a kind of irresistible imperative, Doctor, like Manifest Destiny?"

"How can we not use it, Sebastian? If we know that the human mind can be made kind, benevolent, loving, how can we *not* use it?"

Again, I had no argument. That is, I could not argue in logical terms. I had only the feeling that such power was not the right of any man.

"Sebastian," he spread his hands out before me, shaped out before me, shaped to hold a nonexistent globe, "I don't think you understand how big our organization has become. Soon, very soon, we will have hospitals in every state in this country, and in countries throughout the world. Not designed and built to enslave the world, but to save it from itself; to eliminate from the face of the globe *all* hostility from the mind of a street sweeper or world leader. We can do it. We will do it.

"Again, I ask, why do you wish to leave us?"

"I'm not sure . . ."

"Then, please, join us. *Join* us, Sebastian Cant. Work here at Sunnyview for a new tomorrow. A world of men at peace with themselves and their brothers and sisters. We need you."

"Why?" I was honestly awed by his pleading. "Why am I so important? To mop floors, empty bedpans? What do I have that is so bloody valuable to you?"

"Your mind, Sebastian. Your mind."

"Ha. Very funny."

"Not at all. You have above average intelligence, Sebastian; that is not a common commodity. You could be eminently valuable with a small investment in training."

"Besides that, I know too much to let me walk away. Isn't that true?"

"Not altogether. You ..." He stopped abruptly.

"What? What were you going to say?"

He turned his back to me quickly and walked to the bar, took down two glasses, and pulled the cork on a bottle of Chablis. That bar was his best prop. "I was going to say that you will not leave here with anything damaging in the grasp of recall."

He poured himself some wine and raised the bottle in a silent request for permission to pour one for me. I nodded. The fact that he plainly was telling me that, if I chose to leave, I was in for further brain changing was frightening; but I sensed strongly that he was going to say something else, something more terrible. My suspicions were later proven out ... later when I again met John Macky.

There was nothing substantial decided in Bananastein's office that day. I was merely again on the fence. Here I was a prisoner, and still I was not condemning my jailors. The conflict between my instinctive emotions and my intellectual objectivity was tilting, however, in favor of the latter. I think my long-standing pessimistic view of mankind was the deciding factor. I had always thought he would take the final plunge into the atomic Armageddon. I was always fully confident that somehow the insensitive soul was the most politically successful, and therefore ambitious men of keen minds and oatmeal hearts would always rise to the positions of leadership.

I was convinced that we were a species of killers who would just naturally turn on ourselves when the game ran thin, and here was a man offering a solution, a salvation, as he called it, and he was asking me to get in on the action. A golden opportunity to join up while the mind controllers were in their relative infancy. It was inevitable that they would soon be totally in charge, I thought, and it was coming down to a choice of in or out.

"I think I'll join you," I said, and extended my hand.

"Welcome aboard," he said. I swear he said just that.

I left the office and began a week's involuntary vacation. Bananastein simply made no comment about returning for an interview, and no one else made any demands on my time. I filled the days with golf and random lollygagging, and the nights with Julie. When I asked her where John Macky was and what, if anything, had happened to him, she looked away and said he was fine and not to worry. She, nor anyone else, said anything more, and it was strongly hinted by all that I should quit asking. I did.

Almost a week to the minute since I had last seen him, I ran into Bananastein. I literally ran into him as I bounded into the golf clubhouse on my way to play a solo round. There he was, unavoidably in the path of collision, big as life and twice as hard. I couldn't check my momentum and I knocked him flat on his ass.

"I'm terribly sorry. Are you Okay?" His companion and I struggled him to his feet and there he stood, right in the clubhouse, dressed in casual denims like a person.

"I'm fine," he said, brushing off imaginary dirt. "No problem, Sebastian. No harm done."

Well, I'll be damned, I thought. He's so grateful that I've enlisted in his army, he doesn't even mind if I knock him down now and again. A lovely fringe benefit. "Do you have a moment, Doctor?" I asked. "Would you care to join me in a cup of coffee?" I waved an inviting hand in the direction of the adjacent coffee lounge. He glanced at his companion, who indicated that he could get wherever he was headed alone, and Bananas said yes, he would join me.

We proceeded inside, where we filled Styrofoam cups with hot caffeine at the self-serve counter and searched out a clean table. In the course of these preliminaries I wondered just what it was I had on my mind, and why I had asked him to join me in the first place. As we sat down and seasoned the coffee to our tastes, I found myself panicked that I had absolutely nothing to say.

"How are you doing, Sebastian?"

"Fine. Fine. Everything's just fine."

"Good."

I sipped at my black, sugared brew. He whitened his a bit more with cream. "I'm just relaxing," I said.

"Good, that's good. I add cream just to cool my coffee," he said. "Impatience is my biggest fault. Are you impatient, Sebastian?"

"What do you mean? Generally? Or specifically at this moment?"

"Isn't that the reason you wanted to talk to me, Sebastian? Not, I hope, the reason you knocked me down, but the reason you asked me to have coffee with you? To ask me when you would get started doing whatever it is you are going to do?" That was it, of course. He had scratched the itch I couldn't locate. After the weeks of tense interviews with Bananas and the sobering-up process, I was gagging at the blandness of nonanxiety. After the catharsis, I was suffering from a kind of postnatal depression.

"I think I would like to know what I'm expected to do and have at it. Yes, that's right. I'm ready as I'll ever be and I want to get on with it."

He downed his coffee in one long draught and stood up. "Tomorrow. My office. Nine o'clock?" He placed the feather-light Styrofoam cup on the table and it walked a few inches with a breeze from an opened door. I caught it and crushed it as the expedient way to keep it on the table. "Nine," I answered, and he walked away.

11.

"WHAT time is it?" She spoke into her
pillow without turning up to me, but I understood the muffled question anyway. She
didn't look beautiful in the morning. Her eyes
were the type that redden and collect sleep on
the lids at night. She rubbed at them, intensi-
fying the redness, and sat up. She raised her
fists to the ceiling and turned them in a stretch
that pulled her nightgown taut across her
breasts. Beats the hell out of chirping robins
for a morning starter, I reflected.

"It's early," I whispered.

"Thanks." Her arms dropped and she
scratched her head violently to shake out the
sleep.

"It's about seven, seven-thirty, Julie." She
leaned back on her stiffened arms.

"Where are you off to so early, Seb?"

"I start today."

188

"Start what?"

"I don't know. Start whatever it is I'm supposed to do here."

"Oh."

I finished tucking in my shirt while she got up and out of bed. She was beginning to be beautiful again. She came over to me and put her arms around my neck. "Your breath smells," I said. It didn't.

"It does not," she said, but she wasn't sure. "I'll brush my teeth and start over." She headed for the bathroom and stopped in the doorway, where she reached down and took the hem of her nightgown in her fingers. "Want to see my appendix scar?" Without waiting for reply, she picked the nightgown clean over her head. "See it?" she said, through the sheer fabric pulled tight over her face.

"You have no appendix scar."

She pulled the hem down only far enough to reveal her eyes. "Not even a little one?"

I walked over to her slowly, keeping my gaze fixed on her eyes, until I was standing inches from her bare flesh. She held the gown over her eyes veillike, delighting in her temptress role.

"I'm keeping my head this morning, Salome," I said, snatching out a few pubic hairs to punctuate the remark. She yiped in pain and dropped the gown, calling me a bastard and rubbing where it hurt.

189

I picked up her chin and kissed her.

"You do tempt me, Julie, but I can't let you lure me back under the covers. I need to get into the machinery of Sunnyview as long as I'm joining the club. I'm anxious. So you understand, you gorgeous siren?"

Her eyes brightened, secure in her power. "I'll let you escape me this time, you mere mortal," and she closed the bathroom door behind her triumphantly.

With a yell that I would meet her in the cafeteria, I was out of the room and walking briskly down the hall. This was the first day of ... of what? I didn't know, but I had a familiar sensation of pleasurable anxiety that I hadn't felt since I was young. Summer was over and this was the first day of school.

I missed John Macky. I sat in the middle of the crowded cafeteria amid the noises and suddenly felt plumb sad. I had a fantasy of standing up on a table and announcing to all that I wished to know the saint's whereabouts. Did anyone in the room know? And if they did, would they please contact Sebastian Cant? They could remain anonymous if they wished. I was offering a reward leading to, etc.

Julie entered the room. She was fresh from the shower and was fully beautiful again. She came directly to me and men turned as she passed. I felt a justifiable rush of pride that it was me she was headed for, me, and them she was passing by.

"Good morning, sadist." She flipped her lovely hair back with her hand as she sat down. I handed her a menu.

"Good morning to you, Salome. They're having a special on Baptists today, I believe."

"I'll have a John. On a platter, of course."

"I'll have a John . . . Macky," I said without humor.

Her expression changed instantly. The twinkle left her eyes and her mouth set firm and cool.

"Well?" I raised my voice. "I'll have a John Macky."

"Please, Seb . . ."

"Please, hell!" I *was* getting too loud, and I subdued the volume. "I want to know where he is," I said just above a whisper.

"He's fine."

"Then why won't you tell me, Julie? You profess to love me, but apparently you don't trust me. What is love if not trust?"

"Seb . . ." She put her hand over my fist.

"What?"

"Seb . . . ask Doctor Manna."

"Bullshit!" I hissed, still keeping my voice down. I pulled my fist free of her. "I'll find him. I'll find John Macky." I got up to leave. She was crying without sound. "I'm sorry, Julie."

With the taste of breakfast still fresh in my mouth, I soon found myself seated once again in that familiar Leatherette mother in Bananastein's office. He stood behind me resting his arms on the back of the chair.

"Ready to go to work, Mr. Cant?"

"Not quite."

"Why not?"

"I want to know, first, where John Macky is. I want to see him. I want to talk to him."

"I'm afraid you can't talk to him, Sebastian. He's on duty." As he said this he removed his arms from the chair and turned to walk away patting it as if it were a pet dog he wanted to stay put and not follow.

"I don't believe you, Doctor."

"Why not, Sebastian? Why would I lie? Do you think we have him locked up in a dungeon somewhere? He breached our security, but do you think we had to take medieval steps to amend that? Do you think we killed him? Is that what you think?"

"Maybe. Anyhow, if he is alive, what's the problem? I'll compromise my request. I don't have to talk with him. I'll be satisfied with just seeing him, breathing and healthy. Is that a problem?"

He stood in the middle of the room with one hand on his hip and the other fingering his chin, "All right," he said, nodding at nothing in particular. He walked to the bar.

"Doctor, I really don't need or want a drink."

He held up his hand for patience and pressed or turned something on the wall, which activated a motor mechanism. With an electric hum, a part of the wood panelling recessed and slid sideways to reveal a rather large television screen. Welcome to 1984, I thought. I wonder if we are going to pick up John on the john. No such vulgarity. Instead, the screen flopped this way and that, click, and there he was. He was seated at a console of some sort. He was wearing earphones and looking directly in front of him at the console, while manipulating switches. Our view was slightly overhead and frontal. I wondered if he was aware of our peeping and I asked Bananas if he was.

"He knows there is a camera on him, of course, but he is not aware of its activation."

"How nice."

"The kind of work that Mr. Macky is engaged in carries with it a hazard of falling asleep, as you will discover yourself."

"How so?"

"The activity John is performing is, or will be, part of your duties."

"Which are?"

"You'll soon see, Sebastian." He reached up to turn off the picture and stood up.

"Please, Doctor, leave it on a bit, would you?" I walked over for a closeup look.

"If you like," he said, but kept his hand on the control.

John Macky looked good. His eyes were bright and he was concentrating hard on what he was doing. He would stare ahead then flip a switch or turn a dial to say something. There was no mike visible, but it was clear he was speaking to someone. He was not simply talking to himself.

"No sound, Doctor?"

"I don't have the audio activated."

"Why?"

"We don't eavesdrop without a purpose, Sebastian, and you said you wished only to see Mr. Macky. Well, there he is in living color. Now, are you ready to proceed with the day's schedule? Because I have neither the time nor the inclination to cater to your paranoia."

"Proceed," I said.

"Good." He pressed something and the panel slid back into place and fitted itself forward. It was the work of a craftsman. You couldn't even detect a hairline crack to betray its existence.

It wasn't until much later that I deduced I had seen not live transmission but a tape or film of John Macky.

He closed the drapes, an odd gesture for an administrator, I thought. The more appropriate act of a prissy housekeeper. The man was chockfull of little, surprising idiosyncrasies.

"Shall we go?" he asked, with a look about his arena to see if he had forgotten anything.

"The lamp?" I suggested.

"Thank you," he said, and killed the light on his desk. We left the room, which he carefully locked behind him.

"First stop the zoo," he said, and I guessed that meant the lab and his "friends." I marched alongside him into my new career with feelings of excited anticipation.

"Zoo keeper?" I asked, as I followed him into the elevator.

"Not exactly, Sebastian. In any event this duty will be a minor one, albeit a very necessary function."

The hum that lowered the elevator stopped, then hummed the doors open. Dank . . . a marvelous word. A dank subway. A dank dungeon. A dank Sunnyview basement.

The acoustics amplified our voices and the click-click of our shoes as we marched. One could never simply stroll down such a corridor. The cold, angular structure had a force field that commanded a hurried military strut.

There were other rooms on this level, and as we passed their doors, all of which were metal and painted the same school-gym pistachio with black sequential numbers, I wondered what their function was, and who, if anyone, was busy behind them. Pictures of each interior flashed by like telephone poles from a train window as we walked. A desk here, a table chair, lights on, lights off, a flash of white movement. An orderly? A nurse? Our reflections? Or ghosts?

We reached our goal, the monkey room. As Bananastein fitted his key, I looked up the hallway to our right, then to our left. There was no sound save the distant muffled simian chatter and screeching coming from behind the heavy door we were about to open.

The rest of the floor was dead quiet. Then, as Bananastein held the doorknob in one hand and turned the key in the double lock, a metal door slammed and resounded its way along the cold walls, followed by shoe clicks and ghostly chatter that could have been from another world. Another slam and the walls were silent again. What did those sounds remind me of? A prison. But how did I know that? I began searching my memory in vain and my thoughts were interrupted as Bananas opened the door. The sight and sound of the monkeys was somehow a relief. I felt immediately comfortable among them. Well, hell, that really shouldn't be a wonder, since those animals were more human than most of Sunnyview's citizens. Most notably the wooden heart I was with.

"Well, how are all my friends today?" he asked as he clapped and rubbed his hands together. At the hand clap they set up such a howling, screeching din, accompanied by leaping and shaking of cages, that I thought the hand clap must have been a signal. It was indeed a signal, I reflected, if his cutesy greeting was standard procedure each time he entered the room, and preceded a feeding or something of that sort.

"Are you going to feed them, Doctor?" I yelled above the noise. He shook his head, then yelled.

"They feed themselves!" He indicated a small monkey that was hard at work lifting a round metal bar about a foot long and two inches in diameter. The animal stood up on hairy bowed legs and, like a grotesque miniature strongman, pressed the bar above his head and dropped it onto two metal arms projecting out of vertical slots in the wall behind the cage. When he dropped the bar onto this cradle, the weight depressed it. The monkey then leaped quickly out of the way and two things happened. First, as the cradle lowered under the weight of the bar, a door below it opened to allow a small amount of grain to pour onto the floor of the cage. Then, when the cradle reached its nadir, the bar weight rolled off with a thump onto the floor of the cage.

"Clever?" yelled the doctor.

"Clever!" I yelled back.

"As you can see," he shouted, "each cage has

the same device installed. Look at the gorilla."
Elwood, as I preferred to call him, had a bar at
least three inches in diameter and the width of
the cage. It looked to be solid iron or steel or,
perhaps, even lead.

Bananastein leaned close with his hand on
my shoulder and spoke into my ear.

"That little toy weighs over two hundred
pounds," he said.

"Lead?"

"Lead. They all are." He held up his hand,
gesturing to wait a moment, then crooked his
finger, beckoning me to follow him as he
walked over to the glass cabinet on the wall.
That was where the transmitter was kept, I
remembered. He was going to give them a jolt
of happy juice. A sudden wave of pity swept
over me. It was probably all they lived for in
this unnatural environment.

He leaned close to my ear again as he drew
out his ring of keys.

"They'll be quiet soon and I'll explain further."

He opened the glass cabinet and took out the
transmitting apparatus. He held it in his hand
and flicked the on/off button with a smile and
a wink in my direction. He did so love his
power, the happy bastard.

The room was instantly quiet. The muted
simians were in the throes of pleasure-center

stimulation, and I wondered for a moment what the sensation must be like.

Elwood was sitting with his back resting against the wall of his cage, picking at his knee and making contented sounds in the depths of his massive chest. I liked Elwood. I judged him to be a nice guy who had had some hard knocks. If I were a gorilla, I decided, we could have met in some primeval Eden and become fast friends, pounding each other's hairy backs and slurping at fruit. If he were human, we would share weekends of fishing and cold beer, and I would help him get over the bad memories of his former master.

"Daydreaming, Sebastian?"

"Wondering what Elwood here is thinking."

"He is not thinking, Mr. Cant."

Some of the chimps began to pound the floors of their cages. Pound is really too strong a word since they had no vigor. But what they were doing was a protestation of sorts, like prisoners clattering their cups across their cages; if indeed prisoners ever did that outside of movies.

"What's up?" I asked scientifically.

"What's up is that they want their dosage increased."

"They didn't act this way the last time I was here, and, as a matter of fact, I thought if you gave them only a slight amount you would get inebriation."

"You do get inebriation, as you call it, when the dosage is here." He demonstrated by turning the dial to .25, while holding the apparatus so that I could see the face of the dial.

The patients, or victims, depending on your point of view, began to howl and chatter, while rolling and bumping around in their cages. Elwood was on his feet, holding the bars and swaying back and forth. He bonked his head painfully against a metal crosspiece and rubbed the bloody spot absentmindedly.

"Inebriated is what I would call it, Doctor. What would you call it?"

"Underdosed and dangerous," he said. When the man responded with such remarks he was physically chilling. He turned the dial, still holding the face toward me, back up to .85. Elwood slumped slowly to the floor again and his eyes became glassy. His cousins followed suit.

"We are not quite sure, Sebastian, why the lower dosage produces the active but intoxicated effect, while the higher dosage produces euphoria. We are sure, however, that there is an immunizing factor at work that we did not anticipate. Withdrawing the dosage has, as I have explained, resulted in the patients feeling what amounts to pain, because of the relativity of adaptive conditioning. Do you follow that?"

"I felt sad because I had no shoes until I saw a man who had no feet."

"Exactly."

"You have discovered, Doctor, with your scientific technology, what many a wise man has discerned with observation and common sense—namely, that all pleasure is relative, and therefore so is all happiness. It explains why one man cries over the loss of a ditch-digging job while another leaps from a building on Wall Street because he is faced with the possibility of having to dig ditches for a living."

"Nevertheless, my philosophical friend, electronically produced euphoria is a realized fact, and if we overcome the relativity factor, we will have the power to create a very real heaven on earth."

"What will there then be left to go to, Dr. Manna?"

"What there always was, Sebastian. Nothing."

Elwood grunted at the remark and, when I turned and looked down at him, he shook his head. No doubt in dismay at the doctor's ignorance.

"Will this be my duty, to come down here and give the poor bastards joy jolts? How often? At what voltage? Once a day, or what?"

"One question at a time, Sebastian. This is one of your duties. Yes, once a day for fifteen minutes in the morning, at the same time every day. Constancy is important. A dose each day at eighty-five for this week. Then seventy-five for next week, then sixty, etc."

"Weaning them off, eh?"

"Yes."

"What will be the results?"

"We don't know. That is the reason for the experiment. You are to take notes on their behavior, being very liberal with your commentary. Just tell us what you see. Observe them for about twenty minutes or so each morning and deposit your notes with the nurse in room three-seventeen, on the third floor. Come over here, please."

He led me over to a hip-high console against the wall next to the glass cabinet. The face consisted of rows of green lights with small glass squares next to each one, which were glowing with two-digit computerized numbers. Each green light was identified by a permanent metal number ranging from one to thirty.

Bananas took a clipboard from a hook on the wall above the console. It had a felt pen attached to it by a thin metal chain. There were two small drawers located in the lower front of the console, and Bananastein pulled one open and pulled out the top sheet of a stack of forms. He placed it on the clipboard, handed it to me, and explained its function.

The form consisted of thirty squares corresponding to the thirty lights on the console. At the bottom were blank spaces for my name, the day, and the date, and the time; and a space for "remarks." Each square and corresponding green light on the panel represented a cage. When an animal fed itself by means of the weighted bar manipulation, the act was recorded next to the corresponding cage number. I was to note the number of feedings in the appropriate squares. If the number were three or less, I was to circle the number, and after I had recorded the data, I was to clear the board by pressing the white button marked "clear."

The green light opposite each cage number had a dual function. Illuminated, it meant the cage was, or should be, occupied. A flashing green light indicated a malfunction of one kind or another. It would flash if the cage were not securely locked, or if the feeding mechanism did not perform correctly, or if the water troughs, that were automatically fed, went dry. It would also flash if the sewage system malfunctioned. This system consisted of water pipes that came out of the wall at one corner of the cage and elbowed along the bottom front of the cage. They were perforated and periodically washed the slanted floor with jets of water that flushed waste across the floor into a receiving slot in the wall at the rear of each cage.

If I observed a flashing light, I was to first check the cage doors to see if they were secure, then the floor of the subject cage for moisture and waste matter. The cages were flushed so often that the floors should be constantly wet. A dry floor named the malfunction. If these items were in order, and the light continued to flash, I was to report the matter immediately.

I commented that the designer of the room was a master of efficiency. Bananastein admitted to being the culprit and thanked me for the compliment.

"Doesn't the flushing of the cages also wash away the food?" I asked.

"Yes," he said, "but they are able to feed at will, and, generally, there is so much work involved getting the food they devour it rather rapidly."

"It seems cruel to make them go through so much effort to feed themselves."

"On the contrary, Sebastian, the process serves a multitude of purposes and is, therefore, very efficient. Firstly, they are not likely to overfeed. Secondly, they get an enforced amount of exercise per day, and, thirdly, they are reinforced in the basic stimuli-response conditioning . . . namely, performing an action to trigger a desired function."

"I see," I said, and again expressed genuine admiration for his talents, which he acknowledged with a demure nod in the manner of the seasoned egotist.

Bananastein then asked me if I understood

the form and if I had any other questions. I replied that I did not, and he asked me if I would fill it out as a sort of practice run. I did so, filling in all the appropriate blanks, clearing the board, and signing it.

"Good," he said, and opening the second drawer, he took a sheet from another stack of forms and snapped it onto the clipboard. This form was merely lined paper, again with designated spaces for my name, the day, date, and time.

"This form is for your commentary, Sebastian. If you're wondering why both forms are not in the same drawer, it's to ritualize your duties. Two forms in two separate drawers necessitate two operations. Ritual aids the memory, and, as I said before, the importance of this duty is not to be minimized. Each of these animals represents not only a great deal of care and feeding, but also many man-hours of surgery. They are valuable.

"With this form on your clipboard, you are to inspect each cage and each occupant. Check all doors physically yourself as a backup to the computer. Make as careful an observation of each animal as you can without opening the cages. They can be dangerous. Look for listlessness. Inactivity is a sure sign of ill health."

I eyed him questioningly.

"Of course with transmitter off," he added.

"I should have made that clear. It's a bit noisy, as you know, but you will become accustomed."

"Don't we all?"

"Yes . . . Sebastian, you are to look for inactivity, as I said, and also for bruises or lesions, chafing or skin breaks, or discoloration of any kind. Some of our patients have been known to have seizures of a sort. I have never personally observed one, but I have seen the results. A month ago a spider monkey died of a self-inflicted skull fracture. From the multiple bruises and their age, we concluded the final fracture occurred after many nights of unobserved seizures, and this could have been avoided, as they say in the cancer posters, by early detection."

"Why don't you turn your talents in that direction, Doctor?"

"In what direction?"

"In the direction of a cancer cure. Never mind. It was just an oblique irrelevant thought."

"Let us try to keep our mind on the matters at hand, Sebastian. We have quite enough to concern ourselves with, and it is of no small importance."

"Yes, sir." He could be a very tiring man.

"When you have completed your observations, check the window." He moved over to the only exterior window in the room. It was rather large, about five-by-five feet square, consisting of stout close-set bars and a thick pane of glass on a metal frame. Bananastein flicked a switch of the transmitter and the entire frame, bars and all, slid on tracks into the wall, admitting a draft of air and the sounds of outdoors. It was close to the ceiling and, therefore, when opened, the bottom of the frame was at the outside ground level. Directly below the window on the inside was a series of bars that formed a permanent ladder up to the opening.

"This is the fire escape," he said. "Should you be in this room, or for that matter, on this floor, it will be up to you to save these animals and, of course, yourself."

"Thank you."

"I do wish you would control your immature penchant for sarcasm, Sebastian."

"Sorry."

He took the clipboard from my hands briskly and replaced it with the transmitter.

"These two switches here are the ones we are concerned with." He indicated two marked "Cages" and "Window." It occurred to me that either Bananastein or a helpmate must have had aircraft experience, with the plethora of safety-covered toggle switches at Sunnyview.

"This one," he said, "as I have just demonstrated, opens the window." He flipped it back to "Close" and the thick glass and heavily

ironed window slid shut obediently. "This . . .
opens all the cages simultaneously."

He demonstrated by holding the second
toggle switch between his thumb and forefinger and snapping it to open and back to close
for the space of an eyeblink. Long enough only
to hear all the cage doors emit a synchronized
chorus of clicks.

"The procedure, Sebastian, is to open the
window." He clicked the window switch and
the window slid back again into the wall.
"Then," he continued, placing a hand and a
foot on ladder rungs, "you climb up and out.
Once outside yourself, you use the transmitter
to open all the cages."

"That's fine," I said. "But even if I unlock
all the cages, what guarantee is there that the
animals will then push open the doors and, in
fact, run for it? Have they been conditioned so
that the sound of the locks clicking stimulates
pushing open the doors and bounding out? I
didn't see any make a move for the cage doors
when you clicked them open and shut a
moment ago."

"Very observant, Sebastian. You must
remember that they will be sedated at the time
. . . you will see to that; but once you are out
the window you will dial down the output to
zero. They will all be instantly at peak agita-
tion, and one will push open a cage and be out
on the floor. The others will rapidly follow suit,

and in another instant one will be up and out the window with the rest of them on his heels. Monkey see, monkey do . . . a scientific truth."

"But they'll all be off to the woods and you'd lose them anyway," I said.

"May I say that I am glad to see that you appreciate their value above and beyond any abstract sentimentality, Mr. Cant." Translation: It's nice to see your heart is cooling to our temperature. I wondered obliquely whether it actually was.

"But the answer is in your hands, Sebastian. Just as the responsibility of securing these animals will be in your hands in the event of an emergency. Once they are all out . . . and they will all pour through that window opening in seconds . . . you'll rev the voltage back up and they will stop in their tracks in the euphoria of pleasure stimulation and be recaged with little or no struggle. We have cages stored in a shed just outside the window for that specific purpose."

"How will I know if they have all escaped the room?" I asked.

"They will have. .

"How can you be so sure?"

"Sebastian, with the smell of fire panicking their brains, they would vacate *en masse* in seconds. The probability of stragglers would be minute. With the pleasure feed aborted, the probability is nonexistent."

"Probably."

"Mr. Cant, don't you know that all scientific reasoning is the logic of probabilities, and that all scientific *fact* rests firmly on theories that are considered truths only as long as they are unimpeachable possibilities? If tonight at five P.M. some bright-eyed paleontologist offered unassailable proof that he had unearthed the fossilized bones of Adam and Eve and family, we might at five-oh-one chuck out the presently held theories of evolution in favor of the Biblical Genesis."

He clicked the appropriate toggle switch to close the window and the subject.

"The entire simian population will be out in seconds," he said as the iron frame clunked shut. "You must react at once to dial up the electrical stimulus."

"Before they get out of range?"

"Before they attack someone or get lost."

He took the transmitter from me and asked if I understood everything. I replied that I did, and he placed the transmitter in the open glass cabinet. He stretched out the key from his belt chain and inserted it in the lock on the glass door, but kept his hand on the transmitter's stimulator dial.

"This is the procedure for locking up. In deference to the fact that you are a neophyte and still unused to the cacophony that is a necessary result of aborting the pleasure stimulation, I will close the dial to zero and lock the cabinet as quickly as possible to insure that the sonorous bombardment will be minimal."

I nodded a thank-you and he smiled a mannequin smile. His falsity in all compassionate expression, even this perfunctory show of concern for my discomfiture, reminded me of something observed of a recently deposed politician. A reporter remarked that he was "out of tune with his body."

There in the monkey room I understood what the reporter had meant. Some men are so false that these outward expressions seem to be operated almost remotely, and, the one human expression that must be spontaneous to be genuine is the smile.

At once my musings were halted by the roar of the animals released from their euphoria. Manna moved quickly, replacing the transmitter in the glass cabinet and securing it. In a moment we were outside and he was locking the door on the bedlam.

"To tell the truth," he said, "I don't think one could ever get used to that racket."

"Not to mention the suffering it signals," I said.

But he didn't hear. Or he didn't understand. He clicked on a smile and I returned one, purposefully sardonic.

12.

"DREAM control?"

"Dream abortion is more exact," explained Bananastein in a whisper. We were standing now in a small room similar to a recording studio engineer's booth.

The room was about ten feet square, and was covered, walls and ceiling, with white acoustical tile. The side of the room opposite the entrance where we were standing was entirely console. I recognized it as the same as the one the saint was operating when Bananas tuned him in for me earlier. This, too, had its operator, clad in Sunnyview's eternal white, and busy doing nothing more than scanning the console's bank of lights and occasionally nipping at a cup of coffee.

"Good morning, Ed." The operator did not turn away from the console, but acknowledged the greeting over his shoulder.

212

"Good morning, Doctor."

He then leaned forward, alerted by some signal communicated through the console's maze of multi-hued lights, and spoke into the microphone before him.

"Easy, Thomas. No, Thomas. Wake up . . . put your feet down again . . . put your feet down again, Thomas . . . no, Thomas . . . wake up . . . come on . . ." He was speaking gently into the mike in the manner of an adult to a child, and I had no reason to believe that that was not the case. He pressed a button and the light next to it glowed red for the instant. "That's better, Thomas," he continued, "much better . . . good . . . that's good . . . now up straight . . . no, Thomas . . . up straight . . . please . . . take some water now . . . that's right . . . good . . . some more, Thomas . . . go ahead . . . good . . . stand up, now . . . good."

Bananastein leaned over to me and whispered, "This is what you saw John Macky doing. This is, or will be, one of your main duties."

I looked directly over the operator's head at the tiny electronic Cyclops that scanned him.

"Why is this man . . . this room . . . surveilled, Doctor?"

"A great deal of time and effort would be wasted if he fell asleep. You'll understand why shortly."

The operator continued talking to his

"Thomas," who I imagined to be in a remote room swaying on his feet, groggily trying to obey.

"Good, Thomas! Walk, please . . . no! . . . get up, Thomas . . . get up, Thomas . . . get up, please . . ." He pressed the same flat black button and the same light reddened, only this time an instant longer. "Up, Thomas . . . good . . . good . . . more water, please . . . take the cup . . . more water, Thomas . . . good . . . now walk . . . good—"

He stopped abruptly, his eyes attracted to another part of the console. He flipped a few switches and spoke again into the mike in the same gently prodding voice. "Wake up, Sally . . . wake up, dear . . . this is Doctor, Sally . . . this is Doctor, dear . . . wake up . . . put your feet over on the floor, Sally . . . Sally, wake up . . . this is Doctor . . . you have to get up now . . ."

I cocked an inquisitive eyeball at Banana-stein. He explained, "All the operators are "Doctor" to the patients. It makes for easier transference to the next stage."

I mouthed an "Oh" of understanding together with an appropriate nod. The monkey room and the key flashed to mind for no apparent reason, and I tucked it in a corner for an unbusy better time, but I confess to an orgiastic shot of pleasure each time I thought of

the plan that was formulating itself in the part
of my brain devoted to sadistic satisfaction.

"Do you have an idea of the function of this
room, Sebastian?"

"I think so. The console is hooked to sleeping
rooms housing patients who are awakened at
intervals to keep them from getting adequate
sleep or satisfactory sleep. It quite honestly
looks like a method of torture, Doctor, of the
kind employed in brain-washing techniques."

I kept my voice modulated to the same whisper as Bananastein.

"You are correct, Sebastian, the function of
this room and its operator is to awaken
patients and abort dreaming, but it is not a
form of torture. The relationship is one of Doctor and Patient, not captor and victim. Take a
good look at the board. Observe. I will explain
further when we leave and can talk more
comfortably."

I stood a little closer to Ed. He looked up and
smiled a hello without skipping a beat in his
vocal urgings to his patients.

"One-two-three . . . good, Sally . . . one-
two-three . . . good . . . thatta girl . . . one-
two . . . no, don't lean up against the wall . . .
one-two, come on . . . one-two-three . . . good
. . . two-three . . . one-two . . . good, good . . .
that's fine . . . one-two . . . Okay . . . Okay
. . . fine. Lie down, Sally . . . go ahead . . . lie

down . . . relax . . . good. Thomas . . . wake up, Thomas . . ."

Bananastein crooked a finger and I followed him outside.

"How about lunch, Mr. Cant?"

"Fine. I'm hungry enough."

"Let's go up to my office. We can have lunch brought there and talk in private."

"Room service, eh?"

"Why not?"

I took him in with the corner of my eye as we walked the halls to his office, and wondered how long I would be at Sunnyview, playing pupil to Professor Bananas.

"I'm glad you decided to join us, Sebastian," he commented as he turned the key in the lock of his office door.

I stood in the middle of the room while he telephoned for food, and I felt for all the world like we had just checked into a motel. "Shall I order for you?" he asked.

"Please do," I answered, and looked at the furnishings as if I were there for the first time. He was standing at his desk, which I guessed was an antique. It was large and heavy looking, perfectly suiting to his personality. The bar was a free-standing affair of black Naugahyde and dark wood frame, heart high and six feet or so in width.

As Bananastein ordered Eggs Benedict, I roamed along the banks of books that formed

216

the wall in back of the bar. They were mostly leather-bound medical texts, but here and there a Steinbeck, Fowles, Sartre.

"Soup's on in about fifteen minutes, Mr. Cant. Have a chair." There he goes again, I thought. "Soup's on." So blatantly out of character.

"I could eat a moose," I said, joining in the conspiracy to make him appear folksy.

"I could eat a hippopotamoose," he jested with a wink. I was in danger of throwing up before the meal arrived.

The eggs, toast, coffee, and other hot and warmed goodies rattled through the door on a tinny trolley after Bananastein dropped efforts to be plain folk and returned to the recognizable fish-blooded man of science. A timely change, since it effected the relaxation of my stomach muscles to see him in his proper casting.

"Order," he was saying, "there must be order. The prime requisite of nature is order. Fine, perfectly tuned order is necessary for the function of all life on this planet, let alone the function and survival of man himself." Gee, I thought, I wished he'd ended it with "hisself."

"Uh-huh." I agreed, still forking Benedict. He patted his thin mouth with his napkin and sipped coffee, then patted his mouth again and leaned back. He laid the napkin across his knees, and got on with his pitch.

"Man came along and proceeded to disturb that order, but it will be the scientist who restores order by scientific means, and in a way that will give man the freedom he has always sought. Think, Sebastian, think of all the wasted energy man expends giving vent to his aggresions, his jealousies, his prejudices, his hates. What if he were free of those energy-wasting drives? What then, Sebastian? What material wealth would he be capable of? Imagine how far he would thrust forward and at how fast a rate, if all his energies could be channeled productively! If his hates were abolished, obliterated from his mind entirely, and replaced with brotherly love!"

I had ceased forking and sipped a sip of good coffee.

"You are beginning to sound like a Christian, Doctor."

"Christ *talked* about such things," he waggled a finger. "*We* have the power to see it a reality! Tell me, my eternally moralminded young friend, is it wrong to change men so that they become more Christ-like? By whatever means, is it wrong to bring about a world free of hate and filled with joy and Christian love?"

Damn him to hell. I felt my resolve slipping from my grasp. The pendulum was about to swing once again under the weight of his infernal logic.

"If . . . if it were done with care I suppose. If it were accomplished by . . . that is, if the means to the end are not . . . not evil." He who hesitates defensively opens holes for fifty-yard gains. He drove in.

"That, Sebastian, *that*," he emphasized in triumph, "is precisely the point, and I am glad you used the word evil. We are humans, Sebastian. Ours is a hospital, not a concentration camp. At Sunnyview it is man's pain we are concerned with. We function and survive for the purpose of eliminating pain, and not just physical pain, but the fears and heartaches of man that are unnatural to him, that traumatic experiences generate. Trauma that is recorded forever in his virginal brain tissue. Put there not by genes but by experiences that he has no control over.

"Think of this, Sebastian . . ." He leaned forward, discarding his napkin on the tabletop. He took on the anxious manner of a car salesman about to close a deal. "If we make these changes in the brains of men, using our methods, which are painless and harmless, we can accomplish a permanent change in mankind. We need only change one entire generation. Then we can back away. They will ensure its perpetuation through enculturation of following generations. If you do not believe this then you must by default align yourself with those who kneel at the feet of the negative gods who proclaim that man is at heart an eternally bellicose carnivore doomed to be his own murderer."

Sold, I thought. I'll take the sports coupe with the plaid upholstery.

Crestfallen is the operative label to identify mineself, trudging from the main hospital to the dorm after luncheon with Bananas. The pendulum had swung not entirely over to the doctor, but it had been dislodged from my freedom-bent corner and now merely hung limply in the center. Where was Julie? I felt an urgent need to make love. To mount and hump, and certify my potency at least in that area. I sought her out and found her, of all places, in the golf course restaurant.

"Hello," I said bleakly.

"Oh, hi, Seb!" She turned cheerily away from several whitefrocked swains, clustered around her at the bar. She noticed at once that my woeful countenance bespoke need for mothering, and broke free of her entourage to minister.

"Excuse, gang," she said, and she spun off her barstool throne, drink balanced in hand, and offered me her crooked elbow. She was nothing less than great in the female intuitive art of bolstering the ego of the depressed male. I felt better at once.

"Shall we sit by the window?"

"Okay, Seb. You look a little down, honey. Want to tell me about it?"

"I'll try," I muttered. If my ego factor were up a few degrees I still felt spiritually as limp as an ancient rooster's cockscomb. Perhaps, I thought, a drink or three would put some starch in it.

We settled in, slipping and scooting into a quiet booth by the window overlooking the course. By chance or subconscious navigation, it turned out to be the same table from whence I first spotted the metallic reflections of the evil electronic fence. A good subject to ignite our conversation.

"Do you know, Julie, that Sunnyview is fenced?"

Her eyes showed a hint of fear immediately, and it was awful to see those eyes show that emotion. I was sorry at once for my blunder and frustrated that I couldn't apologize. It was pointless. We were both wearing kits, and even if we weren't, the table was probably bugged. Hell, the place was so far advanced in electronic key-holing the ice cubes in the drinks might be fitted with transparent microphones. I looked into her eyes with apology in mine.

"Of course I know about the fence. Most everyone on staff knows, Seb, and now you are staff, aren't you? Didn't you start today?"

"More or less. I guess I'll actually start tomorrow. Today was an orientation tour. I'll be

221

in charge of the monkey room and I'll also be working in the dream control lab."

"Oh? That's an interesting assignment. I did D.C. for a while . . ."

A waitress materialized at the table, authoritatively halting conversation with her presence as they are somehow able to do. Julie displayed her drink and said she was fine. An interesting idiomatic way of refusing alcohol, I pondered momentarily. I ordered whiskey, specifying no particular brand of poison, just double and tall, as befitting my suicidal demeanor. The waitress floated away with a dribbled "thank you."

"Would it be pointless to say that booze never really helps, Seb?"

"Pointless, but thanks, anyway."

She reached over and held my hand. Presently the waitress returned with her glass-bedecked tray, and lowered a tall one to my waiting free hand.

"Will that be all, sir?"

"Yes."

She was gone and it still felt odd not having to reach for a wallet.

"I still can't get used to the idea of not paying for anything."

Holding her hand with my left, I raised the drink and took a long, breath-taking swallow. Tears sprang to my heated eyes, and I freed my hand of hers and wiped them.

"You ordered double, Mr. Cant," Julie said with a sympathetic smile. I exhaled open-mouthed breaths of air over my burning palate.

"Indeed I did," I said in a voice that didn't immediately catch gear, and relinquished a smile at myself. "You see, Julie, the elixir does work in a back-door way; I'm smiling, am I not?"

I decided to try to erase some of the damage done by my opening query about her knowledge of the fence.

"Julie, I asked if you knew about the fence because I was curious . . ."

Her face blanched slightly and she shook her head for me to stop.

"You were curious," she finished, "about John Macky. Right?" She didn't wait but went on rapidly. It was obvious she wanted to lead me. "It's natural that you would be. John is fine, believe me. I'm sure you'll see him soon and be satisfied that he's Okay. Don't worry, Seb. You worry too much. There's a fence here, sure, but you know every government has security measures, and we're a kind of government. All the good work we are doing here would be in jeopardy if someone with only half truths and paranoid delusions were to leave and bring outside authority down on us. Do you think some local sheriff's department is capable of grasping the profundity of Sunny-

223

view's work or its long term goals? For that matter, do you think the government would understand?"

It was straight party line. She was a good actress and fast on her feet. I answered in kind for our unseen audience, but I allowed my eyes to belie my words.

"I've come to understand more now, Julie, and I know that measures such as the fence are entirely necessary. I have joined; and I realize the ends do indeed justify their means. I *was* worried about John, but if you say he's all right, that's good enough for me."

I raised my glass to her. She squeezed my still-held hand.

"I'm looking forward to tonight, Seb. I'm looking forward to your making love to me."

"This," I said, "is the part where my manhood is supposed to begin pulsing in my eager loins. It ain't."

"Don't worry. It will. Tonight." She winked over her glass, drank a little, and ran the tip of her tongue over her upper lip. Sensuous though she was, I couldn't get my mind off "business."

"Forgive me, Julie . . . I want to know more about the dream control lab. Bananas said he would tell me about its operation, but instead he spent the lunch hour extolling the virtues of Sunnyview. What exactly goes on there? I should know . . . I'm going to operate it, and probably tomorrow." I looked at her searchingly. Had I again stupidly blundered into taboo conversation and put her on the spot? She closed her eyelids for a moment and gave a barely perceptible nod of her head to indicate we were on safe ground. We were saying a lot between the lines with facial expressions. I began to realize that this was the only safe method of communication when one is under surveillance. It was like walking across one of your own minefields. You knew where not to step, but you had better not relax just the same.

"The dream lab." She titled her talk like a high school freshman. "Okay. It's been explained to you, has it not?—the method of excising the unwanted memories? The protein injection at peak recollection, etcetera?"

"Yes."

"Okay. In order to dredge up the memory in the form of a dream, we need a whopper. A scenario as vivid and real as possible. Humans have a need to dream. Not a need in the sense of a need to be loved or a need for attention but in the sense of a need to eat and breathe. It has been learned that if you deprive someone of dreaming he will go bonkers."

"Bonkers," I echoed.

"Absolutely psychotic."

"I see." And I was. I was seeing a facet of beautiful Julie's mind that I never suspected could exist in that frivolous head. Here was

Julie, not the big-bazoomed, dark-haired sensuous sackmate, but Julie the clinical psyche tech. I didn't much like it. She went on, almost by rote, elucidating the operation of the dream control lab.

"Your function as dream control lab technician is simply to prevent the patients under your control from dreaming."

"How do I know when . . ."

"By monitoring REM's, rapid eye movements. You see, when a person dreams—"

"His eyes move," I interrupted. "And when the console signals REM sleep, I electrocute the poor bastard to wake him up, then force him or her to pace his cell and stay awake. Then when he lies down again, I wait for REM sleep to start again and repeat the process until when? Until he goes, as you say, bonkers?"

"You're letting your drink go stale," she said, and her light blue eyes flashed a warning. I took a heavy swallow over my now-immunized palate, and the whiskey made me surrender one of those warm chills that shudder from the belly to the toes.

"No," she continued, satisfied she'd corrected my drift, "we don't allow them to go psychotic. We are not in the torture business."

She was genuinely annoyed and as loyally defensive as a Marxist.

"We bring them to that point, but not beyond it. That is precisely the point at which

226

they move to the next stage. In fact, one of the most important aspects of your responsibility in the DC lab is to prevent them going beyond that point. It is a matter of precise timing, and you will learn all the signals so that you can move them from DC to the next stage at peak readiness."

"Calculated by a computer, no doubt."

"Exactly."

The computer remark was a vain, sarcastic dart, aimed at the dispassionate attitude of the DC lab, but I had been nonfacetious despite myself.

"No stuff?" I asked.

"No stuff." There was a twinge of disdain for my unprofessional slang in her voice that was reminiscent of Bananastein's snobbery and I didn't like it at all.

"I'm sorry if my nonprofessional jargon disturbs you, Julie."

"Well," she said with no apology, "you really should try to be serious about serious matters, Seb."

"I thought you liked my nonseriousness."

"There is a time and a place, Seb."

"I can hardly wait."

"Do you want me to continue, Seb? Or shall we call it a day?"

Right before my eyes, hot-blooded Julie's heart was turning to Formica. All of a sudden I became a little afraid of her. I didn't care how much they talked about adapting to life at Sunnyview. If you were constantly watched and bugged, paranoia was an integral part of the place, and I failed to understand how that illness could be lived with comfortably. The unseen audience, and Julie's transformation from red-hot mama to cold party loyalist unnerved me, and I caved in.

"I'm sorry," I said, hoping she wouldn't salt the wound with, "You oughta be."

"You should be," she said.

I poured an ounce of whiskey over my pride and asked her to forgive my displaced levity and to continue her extrapolation of the DC lab operation.

"I will in a minute," she said, scooting out of the booth. "I have to visit the ladies room." She stood, straightening the wrinkles in her white skirt, and took hold of her kit clipped to her white patent leather belt and brought it from around her side where it had shifted in her maneuvering out of the booth.

"Your clothes get twisted about getting in and out of these inhuman booths," she said.

"Yeah," I agreed, but caught her staring at me hard for the brief span of that sentence and lingering her hand on the kit for a long enough moment after it was readjusted to draw my eyes to it.

"I love you, Seb," she said, her hand still on

the kit, "but you must understand my first duty is to my work here."

"I understand," I said.

She was telling me, I hoped, that her cold party line speech was for the benefit of those ears tuned into our rap session. To make absolutely sure that I understood, she leaned over and, putting her hand on my shoulder, she said, "You're a dear," and kissed me lightly on the cheek, and whispered in my ear, quickly and almost inaudibly, "Fuck Sunnyview."

She straightened up, and with a "Don't go 'way," turned and left for the powder room.

She returned in minutes, but not before I gulped down the remainder of my drink and procured a fresh one.

"I'm back." She slipped into the booth, and with three bounces secured her position near the window. My eyes were warm for her, and I wanted her to see that, so I stared for a moment.

"Well," she said, "I see you have a fresh drink. Where's mine?" She held up a small glass of diminished ice cubes and residual water, which she sucked at with a noisy slurp.

"I'm sorry, I thought I'd wait for you. I wasn't sure you wanted another."

She whirled the ice cubes around by holding the glass by its rim and tracing a circle on the table. "I don't," she said.

Now very much aware of being surveilled,

something Julie was always aware of, I was anxious at the silence, as if we might displease our eavesdroppers by not supplying them with steady conversation. Julie was content to say nothing, displaying no tension, and I speculated on why all spies weren't female, since the softer half of our species seemed to be so apt at intrigue.

"You were saying," I prompted, "that the lab tech's job was to 'build up,' as it were, the need to dream; and that the peak of this urgency was determined by computer?"

"Yes," she said, idly putting down the glass and poking at the ice cubes with her forefinger. I gently pulled away her distracting toy. "Sorry," she said, "yes, the computer is wired into the DC lab's console, which is in turn taped into the patient. It records the number of wake-ups, length of wake-time, length of sleep-time, and most important, interval lengths of wake-ups. It then computes in accordance with programmed formulas and feeds back a signal for the transfer of the patient to the next stage at the appropriate time."

"What is the next stage, if I may ask?"

"Sure. A doctor takes personal charge of the patient and, with hypnosis, directs the patient to remember his dream. He then lets the patient sleep."

"And the floodgates of the patient's id burst open, right?"

"Right. I've listened to some tapes of such dreams and they can be quite unbelievable."

"I would imagine. What if the doctor is unsuccessful, Julie? What if he draws what he determines to be a blank? What then?"

"Back to DC." She saw my brows knit and added, "That seldom happens, Seb, and never does a patient go through DC more than twice. If the doctor doesn't get all he wants the first time, he gets enough to elicit the rest by supplementing the hypnosis with drugs."

"I believe you when you say the patient is not harmed, Julie. I was just wondering how really effective the DC lab is."

"Very effective. When I said dreaming was a need, I meant it, and when you deprive someone of dreaming, the need builds like pressure in a steam kettle or weights being piled one on the other. Eventually, something must give. If the steam isn't released, the kettle bursts. We release the pressure just before bursting point. The intensity, depth, and length of the dreams released are in direct ratio to the length of deprivation. There are, of course, small variations from patient to patient, but the computer takes these data into account and adjusts feedback accordingly."

"Fascinating."

"It is. Truly. DC lab tech is an interesting and important duty. You're fortunate, Seb."

I accepted her esprit de corps as genuine.

No one, I figured, was that good an actress, on stage or off. A conclusion that left me, frankly, not knowing where her loyalties were. I was hopelessly confused.

Soon after her stated opinion that DC lab duty was interesting and important, she left the table. To go on some "short duty," she explained enigmatically. I didn't see her until she slipped under my covers that night.

We made love sans conversation of any sort, and in the morning she was gone from the room before I awakened. When I did, I greeted the morning enthused by the idea of my first official "on duty" day at Sunnyview.

I was scheduled to meet Bananastein at precisely 9 A.M. at the door to the monkey room. I arrived early and stood cooling my proverbial heels outside the metal door, listening to the muted jungle sounds of the bedeviled beasts inside.

Minutes after I arrived, I heard the elevator clunk to a stop, pause, and rattle open its doors to eject what I assumed was Bananastein. The sound of his footsteps increased in volume as he neared the corner which would bring him into my view, but I was not prepared for the man who arrived with those footsteps.

Around the corner came a multi-hued apparition that would have been decidedly more at home coming down the gangplank at Hilo. Coult it be? Yes. It was Beachcomber Bananastein, lacking only a lei entangled in a Polaroid to complete the spectacle. The shirt was the product of a demented silkscreen obsessed with pink flora, and the Bermuda shorts were . . . well, they were a glowing fuschia.

As at the clubhouse, when I first viewed Bananas out of uniform, I could not resolve his dispassionate body in these raiments. My mind simply short-circuited like a computer that has been fed two mutually exclusive facts.

"Good morning," it said as it closed the gap.

"Good morning," I replied, all thoughts of witticism falling short of the live in person joke that hove to my side.

"Put your eyes back in their sockets, Sebastian. There's time for leisure even for me, at our Sunnyview. All work and no play, etcetera."

He drew a key from his pocket and held it up to me in the holy fashion of a corporate president presenting the privilege of the executive crapper to a junior exec.

"Here it is, Sebastian, all yours."

"You don't know what this means," I said with private irony.

"I do. I do. It means you've joined us, Mr. Cant." He modulated his voice to the level befitting the solemn moment. "Joined with us at the infancy of a new, a better world for all men. I want you to know, your decision could not have meant more to me than . . ." He put his hand on my shoulder. O, God, don't say it, I prayed. ". . . than if you were my own son."

"Uhhhh," I said, and drew more hemoglobin from my favorite tongue.

My right hand turned the key in the lock and my left opened the door to bedlam. I crossed the room quickly to the glass cabinet, opened it, and withdrew the black transmitter. I turned around to face my waiting subjects, my hand poised on the dial and I experienced a pleasurable sensation that I didn't care for— all the more repugnant to me because it *was* pleasurable. I was experiencing power. More with that little black box and its waiting contingency of simian idolators than I have ever felt in my life. More than the power over life and death, I, Sebastian Cant, with a twist of my finger, could release these poor souls from purgatory and open the gates of my Father's mansion. The lust I despised in men I was thrilling to, despite myself.

Bananastein, employing the universal windup gesture of ground mechanic to pilot, encouraged me to get the lead out and the juice flowing. I turned the transmitter dial and what was pandemonium became instantly grave-quiet.

"Why did you hesitate so long, Sebastian? I'm beginning to think you *do* like that awful racket."

"No, really, Doctor, I just wanted to . . ."

"To observe the rapidity of the response?"

"Something like that." To savor the moment. That was why I delayed and I cringed at the truth. I was as susceptible to the siren that is power as any man, despite my holier-than-thou derision of its worshippers.

"Good. You are developing a scientific mind. Now, if you will . . ." He pointed to the console, indicating that I should proceed with the prescribed routine of my duties. I removed the clipboard from the wall, glanced at my watch, and jotted down the time along with my name and the date in the appropriate blanks.

After I finished the first form, noting all the figures that measured the feedings, I started on the second sheet, the one used for observational notes. I began with Elwood. The huge gorilla's eyes were glassy, but still held an expression of hate like a wino who is helpless to his need, but despises his condition.

"May I turn the voltage feed down, Doctor?"

"Why?"

"To observe more closely the response."

He didn't like the idea one whit, but how could he refuse a fledgling scientist's professional curiosity? He could not.

"All right. But only for a moment. This really upsets the schedule of input retardation."

"I understand," I said, not giving a damn for anything but reaffirming that half voltage produced drunken monkeys. I turned down the magic dial. The resultant bumping cages and strange chimp laugh-sounds told me that the tribe was at once bombed, but I kept my eyes fixed on Elwood to see exactly at what point he zonked out. He curled his lips grotesquely and gave out a sustained "Uh-uh-uh-uh-uh-uh" that climbed to an ear-shattering shriek. He then fell to the floor and rolled over and over, thoroughly enjoying his cheap drunk.

"What would happen if he were let out in this condition? Would he be dangerous, do you think?"

"That depends on what you mean by dangerous," Bananastein replied testily. The fact that Elwood and his boisterous buddies were not in their glass eyeball state was apparently unnerving him. "Sebastian, if you please," he added hurriedly, as if he had just made me aware of his distress.

"But tell me please," I insisted as I turned the room back again into Zombieville, "would he be dangerous?"

"If you mean would he attack anyone, no, I seriously doubt it. But can you imagine Elwood here, as you prefer to call him, running wild through our hospital with thousands of dollars worth of delicate equipment within easy reach? He would be dangerous, Sebastian. As dangerous, and in the same way, as the proverbial bull in the china shop."

Satisfied, I completed my duty in the monkey room and, accompanied by Bananas, delivered the paperwork to Room 317. Next stop, the DC lab.

There, the duty was about as Julie had explained to me the night before. I got *into* the work, and after a while felt the same ambiguity as I had when operating the transmitter in Chimp City, namely the pleasure of power together with the guilt I felt for enjoying it.

At first I felt sorry for the patients, but after a while I looked eagerly for the REM light to glow and permit me to command my own personal robots. I soon knew all their names without matching card to room number, and called them by their given monikers.

"Wake up, Fred . . . come on . . . that's good . . . feet over the side . . . come on . . ." Being particularly slow to do so, Fred needed electrical prodding, and I zapped him a short burst. It was very effective. As Bananastein had earlier explained, "In the somnambulistic state, even the mild shock evoked by the tiniest penlight battery is quite startling." An understatement, I found. Zap-zap and Fred was up and marching. "That's good, Fred. One-two-one-two." After about the fourth hour and third wake-up, I decided to have some sport. "Bend over, Fred . . . good . . . clap hands . . . good . . . clap one hand, Fred . . ."

"What are you doing?" God said in an oddly electronic voice.

I looked around and saw no one.

"Those are *patients*, Sebastian," God elucidated, clearly admonishing me to knock off the dream lab version of "Simon Says."

"Sorry," I said to the empty air around me. I looked into the inanimate lens staring at me from above my console and speculated on whose larynx delivered the voice of Jehovah, and how many eyes were peering now into my face on which I was wearing my best *mea culpa* expression.

"Er . . . that's fine, Fred. Straighten up, Fred . . . straighten up."

I peered into the television monitor unbelieving. Damned if Fred hadn't fallen asleep in the bent-over position. Man, that's tired, I thought. I zapped him once as gently as possible. The zap receiver was a wireless gizmo inserted harmlessly under the skin at the base of the neck. Either it is a very sensitive spot or the position he was in amplified the effect, because Fred, in that tight cell-like room, executed a back one and a half gainer.

He landed, wedged between the cot and the wall, his inverted face, eyes closed, aimed straight at me with the grotesque upside-down mouth working, "Momma, Momma, I'm dirsty, Momma, I'm very dirsty."

Oh shit, I thought, now I've really had it. The bastard's nightmaring ahead of schedule.

Fred's somnambulistic back flip was the high point of my day, and I regaled Julie with the incident later that evening at supper.

"Was he hurt?"

"No," I said, picking at miniscule oiled and vinegared bits of lettuce at the bottom of a ravaged salad dish. "I'm hungry," I announced, as if my fork poking hadn't made that obvious.

"The steaks will be here soon. Tell me more about Fred. That's hysterical! I did something similar with a ponderously fat girl the first week I was on duty there. Caught it, too."

"Well, you can't get away with very much, can you, since you're constantly in the focus of those unrelenting spy cameras." I clattered my fork onto the plate and sat back to emphasize my disgust at that particular aspect of Sunnyview.

"They have to do that, Seb."

"Why?" I snapped forward in my seat but modulated my second "why?" in reaction to a few nearby turned heads. "Why?"

"To be sure that you don't fall asleep yourself," she said. "That's reasonable, isn't it?"

"I still don't like it, Julie."

"Seb, you can't watch people sleep without it becoming contagious. You can see that, can't you?"

"I suppose, but I still don't like it. I don't like being spied upon."

She rolled her eyes upward, asking a higher court to forgive her impatience.

"I don't like it because I don't like it," I explained.

"That's no reason, Seb."

"Maybe. Does every goddamn thing around here have to have a goddamn scientific reason behind it? I'll tell you something else, Julie: I don't much care for the totalitarian side of *you*, either, and stop acting like a barracks buddy. I like you better as a lover. I had a buddy, by the way. John Macky. Where is he, exactly? Where is he now at this moment, Julie?"

"He's fine," she said lightly, and dismissed the saint's whereabouts with those few words. "Where's the steaks?" she said, obviously not wanting to talk of John Macky at all. Her darting eyes and furtive expression indicated we were in taboo territory. Damn kits. More than inanimate transmitters, they were evil little leeches, alive and clinging and listening.

The waiter arrived, a balding, thickset man who looked out of place among his lean, young workmates. He unsnapped one of those foldable cloth-strapped aluminum horses that serve as tray stands and set down his load. He had only one order, Julie's, which he laid out in careful placement before her. Then he turned to me.

"Mr. Cant, you are wanted in Dr. Manna's office."

My chest went cold again. That was precisely the way they spoke to the saint on the golf course. Not threateningly or even authoritatively, but you plainly understood that it was not a request.

Was this SS goon going to accompany me, I wondered. No. Having delivered his terse message, he asked Julie if she would care for wine or another drink. I excused myself and left for what I was sure was an appointment with doom.

Incredibly, Julie advanced the black-humored advice to "Hurry back." I nodded stupidly and headed for the exit doors.

By the time I reached the main building, I was trembling. Why was I so sure they would not kill me, I thought. Why was I so easily convinced that Sunnyview did not resort to murder? The bastards wouldn't call it that, anyway. It would probably be euphemistically called elimination or termination or eradication or the wonderfully Germanic "solution" to the Sebastian "problem."

I got mad at myself for allowing fear to take possession of me, and switched my fear to anger. Having accomplished the change from a trembling hulk, white with fear, to a trembling hulk, white with rage, I deliberately passed by

Bananastein's office and headed for the elevator, an evil plan fast formulating in my mind.

I poked the heat-sensitive elevator button and waited, pacing to relieve the tension. The elevator arrived with a *ding* and grumbled open to reveal a pretty young thing in starch white, embracing, schoolbooks-fashion, an armload of paperwork. I smiled. Considering my emotional state, it must have come off as one of those crookedy lines that cartoonists favor. She smiled back and asked for my floor while pressing "two" for herself.

"Oh . . . three, please." She obligingly poked "three" to a glow.

"Nice day," she said to the ceiling.

"Yes, indeed," I said to the same spot, and the doors opened and she was off with a "Have a nice day." "You too," I said and watched the doors close on the pleasant picture of her buttocks arguing down the hallway.

Before the elevator reached the third floor, I pressed the emergency stop and then restarted by pressing the button marked "L. L." In a minute the doors opened to the basement.

I hustled down the corridors, panting heavily in the ears of those wicked little men I visualized off in a lonely room somewhere, with their earphones pressed tight to their lobes, sure I was up to no good. They were getting a visual picture, too, from tiny cameras I could spot from the corners of my eyes every few yards as I sped onward.

My heartbeat picked up as I spotted my goal and I pushed through the lockless door labeled "Men," and the inner door into the neon-lit, white-tiled inner sanctum sanctorum. I leaned against the door and rested a moment.

I scanned the ceiling and spotted the inevitable glass eyes. There was one in each corner but the stalls seemed to be out of their vision. Cameras would have had to be perched in the upper corners in order to view their interiors. I entered one and close inspection revealed no camera or microphone.

If Sunnyview was a flawless Utopia, its construction had been in the hands of mere mortals, and, when this particular room was built, some workman left a quarter-inch crack where the side of the stall met the wall. The perfect niche to hold the key to the monkey room . . . to hold this treasure for the time when I would need it to open the door to freedom.

Even though the need was not upon me, I went through the ritual disrobing and seated myself comfortably. With my trousers crumpled around my ankles and my shirttail hiked up and out of my way, I removed the hated kit from my belt as delicately as if it were a live bomb. Once freed, I held it at arm's length, and to hamper the transmission further I closed my hand around it. I was ready. I let a minute, maybe two, slip by without so much as a rustle of clothing. That slice of total silence, I thought, should have the eavesdropping bastards turning dials frantically to see if they had lost reception through electronic failure. I deduced that they would, after some fidgeting, return to proper frequency and raise the volume.

At this speculated point, I began to murmur, mutter, and whisper "the plan." I employed the voices of two of my favorite movie stars in this crapper drama of conspiratorial escape. The impressions were totally unrecognizable, of course, but allowed me the method by which I varied my pitch enough to simulate a two-way conversation.

Even though *they* had undoubtedly seen me enter the room itself, and then the stall, they could not, after all, be absolutely certain that my co-conspirator was not in the twin cubby next to me, having secreted himself there some time before to await my arrival, cleverly keeping his legs out of sight by embracing his knees. There were numerous other possibilities, limited only by the imaginations of my intrepid listeners.

In any case, I was absolutely certain that, whether motivated by genuine concern or plain curiosity, as I diminished the volume of my voice by both lowering it gradually and turning my head away slowly toward the opposite wall, *they* were turning up their volume control in direct ratio, and would have it turned up full when my voice disappeared entirely. I muttered on—"mutter . . . mumble . . . *escape* . . . mutter . . . mutter . . . *tonight* . . . mumble . . . mumble . . . mumble . . . *gun and* . . . mutter . . . mutter . . . *kill* . . mumble *no! yes* . . . *we* . . . mumble . . . mumble . . . mumble . . . garble . . . mumble . . . *here's the plan* . . . mutter . . . mutter . . ."

I allowed complete silence for the time it took me to take a ponderously deep breath and bring the despicable kit, along with the ears of the bastards on the listening end, to a position an inch from my slowly opening mouth and then I let them have it: the loudest scream I had ever managed to produce.

"Yaaaaaaaaaaaaaaaaaasssir that's my baby, no sir I don't mean maybe, yasssir, that's my baby now. . . ." I segued nicely into a lilting whistle as I replaced the little black box on my belt, hitched up my pants, tucked away my shirt, secured all buttons, clasps, and zipper, and stepped out of my little studio.

I was brought up abruptly by my own reflection in the sink-to-ceiling wall mirror. "Well, how are you?" I introduced myself. "My name is Sebastian Cant and I've just sealed my fate."

I then turned to the omnipresent glass eye

eternally photographing this particular dump-room. "Be right there, men. Prepare the rifle team. Remember, one blank cartridge so that no man is dead sure, if you'll pardon the pun, that he fired the fatal bullet."

"Mr. Cant, report to Dr. Manna's office," replied God, right on cue.

"Of course, yes sir, sir. Right away, sir," I said to the camera. I palmed back a wayward lock of hair, straightened my lapel, pulled my white jacket free of wrinkles, and with a snappy Nazi salute, executed a right flank pivot and marched to my fate.

13.

"**GOOD** morning, Doctor," I said, not at all sheepishly. That would have been pointless. He was seated in one of the big black sisters that had become so familiar. The chair was turned out of its normal position to face the door, and therefore me.

He was seated cross-legged, knee over knee, with his elbows propped on the chair arms to allow him to entwine his fingers and rub his chin with his thumbs pensively.

"Have a chair, Sebastian," he said calmly, without changing his pose. There was a definite feeling of finality in the air. A decision had been made, my fate decided upon. There would be no drinks, cigars, or fatherly rhetoric.

I sat, and he said nothing, apparently willing to wait forever for the silence to be broken by me. I crossed my legs and, seeing that it

247

mirrored his pose, self-consciously uncrossed them.

"You no doubt are wondering about my bathroom aria." I mustered up a twinkle to my eye as I said this, and he merely let it hang there frozen in my cornea.

"What shall we do, Sebastian?"

That was it. I mean what kind of decent façade can one throw up after one has dropped one's pants and screamed at the top of one's lungs into a microphone the first eight bars of "Yes Sir, That's My Baby" on a lone commode in a basement men's room. Such a stunt certainly obviated an innocent "What do you mean?"

I was at once as fidgety as a bug on a griddle. I finally steeled myself.

"If you are asking me, Doctor, what course of action you should take, my counsel would be to simply allow me to leave. I would gain nothing by telling anyone about Sunnyview, and you would gain nothing by . . . by . . . doing anything . . . at all." I trailed off.

"Then it's settled then. Is there anything else you wish to discuss?" My entrails were beginning to go cold and my heart picked up its rhythm.

"Yes." I swallowed against a fast drying throat. Panic was at the door and I was barely holding. "I would like to see John Macky if . . ."

He shook his head, aborting my sentence with the gesture.

"Quite impossible, Sebastian." He stood up, slapping the Leatherette arms as he did so. He offered his hand and I found myself shaking it involuntarily. With an arm around my shoulders he guided me to the door.

"Your girl Julie is waiting for you in the dormitory dining hall, Sebastian."

"Thanks," I said foggily. He opened the door and patted my back to send me off down the hall.

"Good luck, Mr. Cant."

I walked toward the lobby, and I was sure that every eye that passed knew what my fate was. "There goes another one," they were thinking. "Poor son-of-a-bitch."

I pushed open the doors and picked up my stride as I crossed the grounds to the dorms. Julie; I was never more anxious to see anyone in my life. By the time I had reached the dormitory entrance I was at a brisk trot.

"I've had it," I announced, coming into the seat opposite her at the small café table.

"Yes, I know," she said.

"Well, I goddamn well wish I had your aplomb."

"Getting loud won't solve anything, will it, Seb?"

"Since you're so bloody calm, would you calmly tell me what they intend to do with your alleged beloved?"

"I'm going to meander over to that coffee urn, pour us both a cup, and by the time I return I hope that you will have attained manly control of yourself." So saying, she rose and made her way to the buffet table.

I knew my overt excited and agitated state was somehow self-generated as a means of displacing the more real sublevel panic that I was managing to hold my foot on. I had to sway topside like a tall building in an earthquake, lest the subterranean tremors crack me altogether.

Julie was winding her way back to me, two cups in hand, tiptoeing and swivel-hipping her way like a matador, allowing the table corners to just miss her soft, flat belly. She heeled down at last and pushed a white ceramic mug toward me, while seating herself with a toss of her hair.

I took the proffered steamy handleless cup. "Whatever happened to the Styrofoam cups?" I said to display my calm nerves, which weren't.

"Special for you, my darling," she tried lightly. "I bribed the coffee maker."

"Special? I've heard of a condemned man's last meal and all the culinary dispensations incidental thereto, but a last coffee break? I'm crushed. Doesn't my impending whatever rate more than that?"

My attempt at humor and bravado was not convincing. Not to Julie. Not to me.

"Why do you go on so?" she said.

"Because I'm worried that I might not go on."

She sipped at the thick-rimmed cup, holding it with both hands.

"What exactly did Dr. Manna tell you about your future?"

"Nothing. I simply suggested to him that I leave Sunnyview and he simply replied that it was, quote, all settled then, unquote. Julie . . ." I pulled her wrist gently, lowering the coffee cup she held to the table, "I want you to tell me something. Something I know you're not supposed to tell me . . ."

She raised the cup to her lips, dragging my hand along with it in an effort, it seemed, to bury her face and avoid not only what I was saying, but my eyes, too.

"The bloody damn kits! Here, you can have mine!" I wrenched it free of my belt and handed it to her in the manner of a policeman turning in his badge. "I'm resigning. To hell with my pension!" I added, to keep the dialogue appropriate to the drama. And slapped the thing on the table.

She could not have been more horrified had I laid van Gogh's ear on her placemat.

"You . . . you . . ." she fumbled.

"So what? Have I placed myself in any

greater jeopardy by this little symbolic ritual? Should I concern myself less with the retribution than the cause? They can only hang me once, lover," I concluded, with the sudden fearful thought that at Sunnyview they may have even worked *that* problem out. My insides were chilling again rapidly, but I wouldn't strap on that kit again. That little black parasite, I decided, was detached from me for good and all time.

"You keep yours on, Julie. It will, after all, function for both of us." I sat back with this pronouncement, making the most of my now superior position of freedom in contrast to hers. A façade, of course. My nerves of steel were, more descriptively, as firm as cooked linguine. I suddenly felt the need for fresh air.

"Julie?"

"Yes?"

I stood up. "How about catching some starlight. Okay?"

She nodded and rose.

Once outside in the cool evening air, I relaxed a little.

We walked, I with my hands plunged into the side pockets of my jacket, kicking a stone every other stride, and she with her arms folded against the chill.

"S-s-s-cold," she said, and pushed one arm through the meager space between my arm and my side. She hung on with both of hers, and we strode down the blue-gray path to nowhere in particular.

"Cold nights make for bright starlight," I commented, going off the path to kick a particularly kickable stone and dragging Julie with me. "In fact, cold and beauty are very compatible. Everything looks better in the cold, from landscape to the female complexion."

"And the male?"

"I don't know. What do you think?" I said, throwing her a profile.

"Like a rose petal. Freeze-dried, of course." She was again my lover. There was no further mention of Bananastein nor speculation regarding my fate at Sunnyview. Instead, we talked of love and the weather and love and poetry and Frost's reference for heat in his "Fire and Ice."

Julie started the poem, but before she finished the first line, both of us, having the simultaneous urge and communicating the need with a glance, began a hustled walk back to the heated dorm. Panting out the poem as we strode, the cold wind to our backs, and the envisioned fireplace goading our steps, she sang:

> Some say the world will end in fire
> Some say in ice.
> From what I've tasted of desire
> I hold with those who favor fire

"Something, Something, Something. What, Seb?"

"Something about ice would suffice," I answered, just as we reached the doors of the dormitory. We headed straight for the Winter room and the fireplace. There, we were fortunate to find a vacant wing-back close to the hearth, large enough to accommodate both of us snugly.

"I must look up that poem," she said almost to herself, "to see how it does end. Things like that bother me. I once stayed up all night trying to think of an author's name. I can't stand it if I know something but I can't recall . . ."

She squirmed in my lap and I brought her head closer. "You know Julie," I began, then stopped. "Damn, I wish we had privacy. That damn receiver your wearing. The bloody thing is actually, not symbolically, although that's true enough, but actually, sticking in my side."

"I'm sorry," she said, and lifted her hips, shifting the weight off my side where the kit dug into me.

"Better?"

"Thanks."

"You know, Seb, they don't listen all the time."

"How so?"

"Well, I know a fellow who has that duty."

"An eavesdropper?"

"It's called Security."

"It's eavesdropping, keyholing, voyeurism. A nose by any other name."

"He's really a nice guy. It's just another duty."

"Yeah, well. You say they don't always listen? Tell me more about that. That I'm interested in."

"They don't listen . . . they don't listen when we're making love."

"How do you know that? You have only one guy's word for it and he may be lying. In any case maybe *he* doesn't but he may be the modest exception."

"No. He wasn't lying. I know."

"How?"

She didn't answer.

"You and him?"

She nodded.

"He made love to you?"

Again she nodded.

"Pardon me if I don't appear crestfallen, since my crest don' have no more fall, and all that."

"It was before you, Seb."

"Ha! Before Sebastian. That would be B.S., wouldn't it?"

"Not so very funny. I was trying to salve your feelings."

"I think a drink would be in order, Julie. How about you?"

"Yes. I'll get them."

She unwedged herself from our upholstered womb and stood up. I grabbed her hand as she started to go.

"Will they really leave us to ourselves then? When we . . ."

"Make love? Yes."

She freed the kit from her belt and held it to her mouth.

"They're not creepy types who nose for the sake of nosing," she said, directly into the kit. "They're just doing their job and they realize making love is no breach of security."

She hooked it back onto her belt and with a kiss on my cheek was off for the booze.

The hour was late and I was tired, and therefore the drinks were doubly effective. In short order we were climbing the stairs, I under partial sail.

"You know," I said as a drunk utters that phrase, two octaves above normal pitch, "*I* want to know how the poem ends. I wish to procure this infamashion. I like poems and stuff," I slurred.

"Sure, Seb. Tomorrow, Okay?" She had one arm around my waist while I had one anchored over her shoulder. With her free hand, in a succession of grabs and pulls at the banister, she towed us both up the stairs.

"Where?"

"Where what, Seb?"

"Where can I get the infamashion 'bout the poems?"

"In the library."

"What liberry? Is there a liberry in this place?"

"Yes. Come on, Seb, you're heavy, honey."

She managed to lead me down the dim hallway to my room.

"Where is the liberry?" I asked as she undressed me.

"It's on the second floor, main building," she said.

I tried to make love to her but lost the battle for potency to the wilting effects of intemperance.

I came out of my sleep sitting up and rubbing my eyes and forehead with my palms. Julie was propped head on hand on elbow, lying back of me.

"What time is it?" I asked, posing the hungover drunk's eternal first question.

"Too early. Come back to bed, honey."

I think she wanted me to resume the previous night's aborted mission, but my head hurt and I had a stomach threatening the morning awfuls. I needed air and stood up a bit too quickly, nearly passing out in the process. I held my head securely to prevent its falling off and rolling across the floor and I groped my way to the window, ignoring the pleas of Julie to return to the sack.

The windows of my room were the kind you wind a handle to open. I proceeded to do so.

Before the window was half open I saw him. There he was, big as life, standing at a window directly opposite mine, clearly visible from the waist up and looking straight into my soul. I waved. No response. I waved again more frenetically. It was John Macky, alive, and not fifty yards from where I stood.

Perhaps, I thought, though facing me head on he is actually looking away, or at the ground below. No, He *was* looking at me. I could feel it. Why did he not wave back? I cranked the window fully open. I cupped my mouth and was about to yell his name, when he did something strange. He looked behind him to satisfy himself that it was indeed him that I was waving to, and only then did he wave back. He could see me as clearly as I him, yet he didn't recognize me. That seemed to be the only explanation. Why? My mind darkened with imagined possibilities.

I turned quickly and went to the bedside, where I gently shook Julie, who had re-entered Nod.

"Honey. Honey, wake up."

She groaned as she rolled over on her back and looked up at me, shielding her eyes from the sunlight. "What do you want, Seb?" She patted my hand and rolled back on her side. "Come to bed, Seb," she invited.

I took her shoulder in hand and pulled her around to face me again. "Julie. Do you know who I just saw?"

"Who?" She was awakening fully now, and because of some instinctive impulse, I decided not to tell her about John Macky.

"Where is the library?" I asked, hoping she didn't grasp what I had previously said.

"Who did you see?"

"What do you mean?" I asked.

She sat up yawning, stretching, and rubbing her eyes free of blurred thinking. She shook her head to complete the ritual.

"Didn't you say you saw someone?"

"No," I said with wide-eyed innocence. "I asked you where the library was."

She pulled her legs up under her to sit cross-legged and gave her full mane another shake.

"I must have been dreaming."

"Yes."

"The library?" she yawned.

"Yes. I want to see if I can dig up that poem we were trying to remember last night. You know. Frost. " 'Fire and Ice'?"

"Oh, yes," she said, spilling her legs over the side of the bed and standing. "Second floor. End of the north wing. Or is it the east? . . .

259

Well, anyway, when you get to the nurse's station on that floor, ask."

It was the second floor Macky was on, or the apparition of Macky. I grabbed her head in both hands and kissed her a violent smack on the lips.

"Thanks, hon."

I dressed very quickly while she occupied the bathroom and was out in the hall in seconds.

I took the stairs two and three at a time, paused before the mirror in the first floor hallway for a momentary final check, pushed open the dormitory's front door, and headed for the main building. I continually wiped my palms on my uniform as I walked. I was scared. Not so much of being caught, but rather of what I suspected I would discover when, and if, I cornered John Macky. Perversely the fear was drawing me to its source rather than repelling me. I had to know the worst. To see the living, breathing proof of the evil I could smell in the air of the place. They could kill me or do whatever they liked, but before the finale, I had to put my hand in the fire and touch and feel the truth.

I rounded a corner and God Almighty if Bananastein wasn't standing there not ten feet away from me waiting for an elevator. He had his back to me and I froze like an animal lest a sound turn him in my direction. I realized at that moment how much I feared the man. I backed up slowly not taking my eyes from him until I was back around the corner, gathered myself and retraced my steps, half decided that I would abandon my quest.

But somehow the near confrontation and the resultant fear strengthened my resolve. I spotted a door marked "Stairs" and I pushed through and bounded up the steps. I burst out into the second floor hallway with such abandon that I collided with a woman who happened to be passing the doorway at that unfortunate moment. I grabbed her to prevent her being knocked off her feet. She was obviously a patient, dressed in a blue terrycloth bathrobe and disposable hospital slippers. When I grabbed her she set to laughing loudly and uncontrollably and pounded my chest in accompaniment. A nurse appeared, and taking this woman by the arms from behind, pulled her from me.

"Calm down, Sarah, calm down. Come on, dear. We have to go back to our room now." The nurse shot me a look that questioned whether I had a right to be breathing, much less near her patient.

"I'm sorry. I'm lost. I'm looking for the library." I said.

"Are you assigned this floor?"

She cased me head to toe.

"No. DC lab tech. Doing research . . . for Dr. Ban . . . for Dr. Manna."

Suddenly, I instinctively felt that I was being surveilled. A quick glance ceilingward revealed a camera moving back and forth on a pivot in an arc that scanned the hallway. I had little time, that was for damn sure.

"I thought it was up this way," I said, and rather than use a finger to point, I turned my whole body to face the opposite end of the hall and thus throw my back to the camera as it reached its apex, and began its return trip. There was a chance it had not as yet seen my face.

"Yes, it is down at that end," she said testily. "Clear down. Through the large double doors."

"Thank you," I said, keeping my back to both her and the camera.

"Come on, Sarah. Come on, dear," I could hear her say as she guided a mildly protesting Sarah back to from wherever she had strayed. I spotted another camera tracing its searching arc across the corridor and I genuflected quickly to untie and slowly retie a shoelace. I bent my head down and out of view, in full concentration to the task.

I raised my head tentatively and found that I had timed the camera's pivoting pretty well. The little black spies were located about every thirty to forty feet and pointed downward at about a forty-five-degree angle, each giving a scan of a chunk of hallway. Also, whoever in-

stalled them was nice enough, or careless
enough, to have set them to sweep their arcs in
unison. Thus, once one got the timing down,
one could avoid giving the camera a decent
view by evasive strategies. This I did by
making my way in a snakelike pattern, down
the corridor, door to door, first to one side,
then the other, peeking through the small
chicken-wired glass windows, hopefully appearing to be lost and always presenting my
back to the cameras.

Periodically I would fall to my knee to at-
tend my shoelaces, or feint a sneeze, hands to
face, or rub my forehead with splayed fingers
in deep and sudden thought as though trying
to recall something of import. But I could only
continue these tactical machinations for so long
before appearing to either be possessed of a
spastic disease or, more likely, to be deduced
as a fugitive avoiding the electronic onlookers.

Convinced that the jig was about up anyway,
I peered, palm over eyebrow, Indian style, into
the small wire mesh glass in the last door at
the end of the hall. There he was. I opened the
door and stepped inside, sure that I had but a
few panicky minutes before the storm troopers
would pour in upon me, or the P. A. system
would beckon me to Bananasville.

The room I had entered was quite large:
roughly thirty feet in depth from the wall of

the door closing behind me to the outside windowed wall that I faced. That wall had as
much window as wall and presented a view of
the grounds, including the dormitory from
which I had espied the saint earlier.

The room was longer than it was wide. A
good fifty feet or more, I estimated. It was
pink, or one might opt for coral—nonetheless,
a pastel shade in disconcerting contrast to the
ceaseless white of the rest of the hospital.

There were card tables and their accompanying folding chairs, at which sat a variety of
souls all wearing uniformly blue terrycloth
bathrobes and white slippers. The room had
the flavor of a convalescent home with a con-
tradictory factor: There was apparently no one
physically disabled and the older people were
in the minority. Still there was that flavor.
Perhaps it was because they all seemed to be
engaged in what is the most popular and ironic
endeavor of old folks' homes, namely, killing
time.

I was struck by the lack of attention I received. The manner of my entry (hurriedly
stepping inside and moving no further), and
the fact that my expression was probably one
of anxiety if not panic, should have drawn at
least a few curious stares, but no one paid me
any mind all.

The room was dominated by what appeared
at first to be a four-sided traffic light. It had

yellow and green lights on each side and except for the fact that the red light was absent to complete the usual triplet, it was of the same size and general design of a city traffic light. It hung in the center of the room, about five feet from the ceiling, strangely utilitarian in what was otherwise a comfortable-looking game room.

John Macky looked at me.

He was seated at a long table along with several other blue-robed inmates, working on what I saw was a large jigsaw puzzle. When his eyes met mine I broke into an immediate grin, which he returned with a cheerful smile. Every muscle in my body relaxed in response to the evidence that he clearly recognized me. I moved at once toward him, but, as I did so, an odd mixture of fear and hurt changed the look in his eyes.

I sat down in the vacant chair opposite him, reaching over the table an open hand of greeting. He shook my hand firmly but said nothing.

"Hi, John, you old son-of-a-bitch," I said, holding my voice down to suit the library atmosphere. He smiled weakly.

"Hi," he said.

I shot a quick look around that line where the walls meet the ceiling, and saw the inevitable camera scanning the room. I expected to have only minutes before the Gestapo entered and I decided that I would be best advised to spend my time in fruitful conversation since looking for the arrival of the inevitable interruption would not stave it off, much less prevent it. I leaned over closer to the saint.

"You look great," I said.

"Thanks," he said flatly.

"Well? Whatcha up to? What gives?"

"I'm fine," he said.

"All right, you're fine, but what else?"

"I don't understand. Are you here to examine me?"

I stared without answering. I looked long and steadily into his eyes, and the truth came over me with a feeling of profound horror. I was a stranger. As totally a stranger as if we had never exchanged a glance. The truth was obvious but I asked the question anyway:

"You don't know me, do you John?"

His eyes grew wet and brimmed, and a single perfect tear ran down his ruddy cheek and he wiped it away with his fist.

"You know I can't remember!" he said as a child would whine to an impatient father. "You know I can't!" he whined again. He shot a glance over my shoulder and somehow I knew he had looked at that odd fixture hanging in the middle of the room. I turned to look at it again myself, then back to the saint. He was rubbing his reddened eyes. I pulled his hands gently down.

"John, why are you looking at that?" I

nodded my head in the direction of the traffic light.

"I don't know," he said weakly, making no effort to free his hands though I held them loosely. His whole demeanor was one of total submission. I let go of his hands and he began turning over pieces of the jigsaw puzzle from picture side to blank side.

"How many times have you put this puzzle together, John?"

"I don't know," he said, beginning to sob. "Are you examining me? Is this part of the examination?"

He looked at the traffic light again. I noticed several others at the table shooting glances at it as they idled their time at chess, cards, checkers, and the like.

"What's with that light, John? Why do you keep looking at it?"

"I don't know," he said. "I don't feel good. I'm nervous." He was looking at me as he said this, but abruptly he looked up again at the odd chandelier and just as abruptly the room was astir with people getting up, putting away books, cards, and other paraphernalia. I turned around my chair to see what was the cause of the disturbance and my eyes were immediately attracted to the traffic light. The yellow "Caution" light was aglow. When I turned back John was gone. All of the blue-robes were seating themselves in easy chairs. I hadn't no-

ticed before but, unlike the straightback
chairs, the upholstered ones that were scat-
tered about the room were all facing the center.

Suddenly, the air was filled with a clear bell
tone. More human than electronic, it sounded
as if a coloratura had hit a note in the high
register and was sustaining it beyond human
capability. At the same time the light turned
green and my heart went stone cold dead at
what I saw.

They were all moaning softly in their chairs.
Some, legs stretched out, arms folded gently on
their chests; others, curled up, head against a
wing-back's sculptured side. And all of them
with half-wit grins dressing their otherwise
blank faces.

I looked around quickly to John Macky. He
had ensconced himself in a particularly full-
bodied velvet easy chair, close to the center of
the room. I walked over to him and looked into
blue eyes that stared back, seeing, but not car-
ing what they saw.

As I backed toward the door I spotted it on
the side of his head. A dime-size circle of hairless skin with a black metallic dot in the center,
just above the ear back of the temple. This was
the monkey room, only these were human be-
ings. I turned and ran; the coloratura's note resounding and sustaining still as I fled in horror,
barely making it out into the hallway where I
vomited uncontrollably.

14.

"DON'T move!"

Dr. Manna froze. I had no weapon with which to cause such an intimidated response, but he reacted as suddenly and submissively as if I had a pistol pointing at him rather than my finger. My corpuscles were inflamed with adrenalin and Bananas could see the violence in me.

"Doctor, he knocked me down . . . he . . ." It was his nurse speaking. Standing beside me, capless, her hair disheveled and her voice wavering with the tremolo that precedes tears, she tried to collect herself. "What should I do, Doctor?" she asked. "Should I call . . ."

"No!" I ordered. "Don't call anyone." Bananastein stood still, hand out of view behind the desk—perhaps on an alarm button. I had stiff-armed the nurse when she tried to stop me from entering his office. She had crashed against the wall violently and fallen to the floor, and then had fumbled to her feet and trailed in after me.

I was rooted to the spot, my arm iron-stiff pointing the finger that held them still.

"If you move, or if she does, or if anyone comes through that door, for any reason, I will be on you in an instant and I will twist your head until I hear the crunch of your neck bones if it is my last act on this earth. I will do it with such violent swiftness, no one will save you."

He straightened up, very slowly, lifted his hand from behind the desk, and slipped it into the side slash pocket of his smoking jacket. Having done so, he allowed his body to slacken and relax until the pose was transformed from one of arrested urgency to casual aplomb.

Fearful that if I mirrored his relaxation I would lose the intimidating power I held, I remained welded in my aggressive stance.

"It's all right, Mary, please don't be upset. Mr. Cant won't harm anyone, I assure you. Please return to your desk and don't call anyone, I mean that. Mr. Cant and I will chat, won't we, Sebastian? There is nothing to worry about. I'll call you if I need you."

I kept my eyes on Bananastein but I could catch the nurse in my peripheral vision and feel her sizing up the situation. She didn't want to leave us alone no matter what the doctor said.

"Go on, Mary. It's all right," he again reassured, and with a "Yes, Dr. Manna, if you're quite sure," she left the room and it was very quiet. I at last lowered my arm and forced my muscles to slacken somewhat, but the blood was still in my face and blind hatred was still gripping me.

"I saw John Macky, *Doctor*." I snarled the title. He leaned back, his rump against the desk top, and folded his arms.

"That's unfortunate," he said, and his eyes lowered to the floor on a spot midway between us.

"How inhuman you are, you creep, that you could dismiss that awful meeting with the term 'unfortunate.'" I moved closer to him and he raised his eyes to me and stiffened a little.

"I mean unfortunate in the sense that you saw him cold turkey, as it were, without explanation as to the ..."

"Explanation? In the name of God in Heaven, what could you possibly explain? How could you *do* it?" I raised my hands to the heavens in supplication. "Why didn't you just kill him?"

I could feel the tears brim over and stream down my cheeks, and I grabbed him by that pretty jacket of his with both fists.

271

"Why didn't you kill him, you goddamn monster?"

I wept. Bananas's body went stiff as a board in my hands and his face blanched of color. It suddenly occurred to me that more than murder the bastard, I wanted to speak my mind, as if that would be the greater punishment. I released my grip and turned and walked a few paces to allow him a respite.

I turned and pointed my finger at him again.

"You just stand right where you are, dirt. I want to tell you a few things."

"Go on," he said shakily. But he was obviously relieved that I had gained some measure of control over myself, and he wanted to encourage me to continue to do so. His cheeks began to recolor with the knowledge that he was no longer in danger of being strangled, at least not immediately.

"Go on, Sebastian. I am interested."

"You know why I call you Bananastein? Do you, Doctor? Because you're possessed by the same obsession as the lunatic scientist in that lovely tale. You and every goddamn power-lusting scientific creep like you—all suffer from the same maniacal imperative. It's a disease as true as any mental illness and more destructive than most.

"You are possessed by the Frankenstein Imperative. Shall I define it for you? You cannot resist the temptation to manipulate that which can be manipulated. You cannot let lie the reins of any power you discover can be bridled. You *must* open the Pandora's Box if you find the key, no matter what evils may be unleashed upon your innocent brothers. All of this you do under some aegis of holy appointment to discover the mysteries of the universe. You take the bravado of the mountain climber who gives as his motive the fact that 'it is there,' and apply it to the pit of Hades. You're the one who eats of the fruit of knowledge, determined to make a hell of whatever Eden there is still left in God's world. You gorge on that tree in your self-ordained blessed quest, and you vomit up the Hiroshimas and relieve yourself of any guilt because you didn't fly the planes or pull the trigger on the bomb bay door."

"That's quite a speech, Mr. Cant. You ..."

"I'm not through yet, worm." He shrugged his shoulders but he was scared.

"Now you're engaged in the most sinful activity of all. You invade, you *dare* to invade, the sacristy of the soul. If ever the devil himself has tempted you and your ilk to trespass you are doing it now. Here at Sunnyview. That name! Hah! How ironic. The view from here for mankind is hardly sunny! It is the blackened view of hell on earth I see."

He said nothing for a moment. I was spent and the room suddenly quiet as a grave.

"Sebastian, you believe in God, don't you—

the kind old man with the white beard?" He smiled.

"Perhaps. I don't know. But a power beyond this life. Beyond what we can see."

"Christian?"

"I believe Christ's teaching to be the only true salvation of man, if not mankind."

"That is where we differ, Sebastian. There is no God."

"You mean you don't believe in God."

"Belief, my dear Mr. Cant, to a scientist comes only after the proven fact. There is no God. If you think of me as the Adam of the garden, who fell from so-called grace by eating of the fruit of knowledge, then you are the child of that garden who never grew up. In your eyes I am a monster and you are the golden-haired hero. In my eyes I am a realist and you are an infant living in a world of childhood fantasy. If it were left to your sort, the world would remain forever in the dark ages of ignorance."

"If you have your way, we'll move into a dark age of Godless inhumanity."

"Then it's a stand-off, Sebastian. What it comes down to is merely a matter of opinion, is that not so?"

"No. It is not simply that."

"Why?"

"Because, Bananastein, I believe in the free agency of man. His God-given right to choose.

To believe or not to. To decide with his will and soul. I don't wish to force my will on yours, but you wish to force yours on mine. And that is all the difference in the universe."

"We will win, Sebastian. It is inevitable."

"Not me. Not me, Doctor, because of what I hold here in my hand."

I walked over to him, holding my closed right hand out to him, and his eyes followed my fist all the way, I think, until it connected with his jaw. He flew up against the window from the force of the blow, through some miracle not shattering the glass. His flailing hands clutched at the drapes in reflex and dragged them from the rod in a heap on his crumpled body. I bolted from the room, and in my flight once again knocked over the hapless nurse.

I careened down the hallway handspringing off walls to make the corner turns without slowing down. Midway along the first long corridor a nurse slowly pushed a high tiered cart across an intersection and put her hand to her mouth as she saw that I was not going to slow down, much less stop. I couldn't. My momentum was too great. The best I could do was turn a shoulder to it at the instant of collision.

It must have been a spectacular crash. The cart was almost the breadth of the hallway and about my height. It consisted of about five or six shelves loaded with a mass of bottles of all sizes containing liquids of various colors. The cart was of a flimsy, tinny construction, which helped to absorb the shock of the impact without breaking bones. Had it been of a more solid construction, I'm sure I would have been badly injured. As it was, I sustained bruises and cuts the length of my torso and right arm, a large lump on my noggin, and crushing frustration.

Two strongly built orderlies dominated the crowd scene that generated from nowhere and half circled me as I lay among the debris. My white uniform was suddenly multi-colored by the various liquids of my target and splashes of my own hemoglobin. The rack lay on its side. The prevailing odor was rubbing alcohol, and when someone said "Get a doctor," I laughed, increasing the pain in my bonked head.

Someone said, "Here comes Dr. Manna," and the two orderlies did not turn to look as did the others. These two stood, arms folded, elbow to elbow over me, and the thing I noticed most about them was their massive forearms—a requirement for Oriental palace guards and eunuchs who protect the harems of fabled Eastern potentates. That's what these two meatballs were: the sentries that trapped the invading Baghdad thief. The Gestapo that cornered the fleeing Jew. The Mafia goons awaiting the commands of their lieutenant. All cut from the same mold. Then their master arrived, nodded approvingly to them, and kneeled over me to minister.

He reached under and probed the back of my neck with his fingers. "That hurt?"

"Fuck you."

"Roll him over on his back, Charles," he commanded the blond eunuch. "Be gentle."

Charles rolled me over and he was not gentle. He couldn't be. He was designed for moving Steinways, not injured patients. I moaned as pain sparkled from each of my many bruises and lacerations.

"Well, you haven't broken anything vital, Sebastian," Bananas said.

He nodded to the two goons. They could go now. Their quarry was well in hand and theirs was a job well done. Two other orderlies materialized with a gurney stretcher and the gaggle of onlookers parted to admit them. They lowered it to floor level on its expanding-contracting legs and lifted me onto its sheeted soft pad. Moving quickly, they secured me with straps and I began another ride. The ceiling turned one hundred and eighty degrees and then began moving rapidly. The smell of the hospital was strong in my nostrils, mingling with the aftershave of the orderly immediately over my head. I lost consciousness.

"How are you feeling, Sebastian?"

My eyes opened to another ceiling, this one unmoving. The voice had come from the foot of the bed on which I now lay. I jerked my head up and when I did, pain pinpointed the lump on my skull and I groaned in response. It was Bananas all right, straddling a wooden chair, looking over its back which faced me. It was a way of sitting in a chair that always seemed to me to have some kind of pointless significance.

"How are you feeling?" he repeated. I let my head fall back on the pillow and resumed gazing at the ceiling, unanswering.

The door opened and the face and white cap of a nurse came into my field of vision.

"Not now, nurse," Bananas said, and the nurse turned and left. The scrape of the wooden chair legs told me he had risen to his feet and the upper half of him floated into my ceiling scene.

"That was quite a spill you took." He smiled down at me.

"Thank you. I loved it myself."

He forced his smile to broaden in appropriate response and as I stared back up at him I became fascinated by the view of the mouth from that inverted position that causes normal over-bite to become grotesque under-bite.

"It was stupid of you to strike me," the monster mouth said, "and equally stupid to think for a moment you could simply run away." The inverted mouth bit the upper lip and a hand tenderly rubbed its chin. "You pack quite a punch," it said.

"Thank you again. You're taking it quite well, Doctor."

"No, I'm not," the mouth said, becoming more hideous with the change to hostile tones. It bent over me, closer.

"You will soon be watching for the green light with your friend John Macky," it said.

"You savor that idea, don't you, Bananastein?"

"You had every chance, Sebastian."

"Perhaps. And perhaps you are going to do what you feel must be done for the security of Sunnyview, and the continuance of your noble work, but the fact is, Bananastein, you are obviously enjoying the punitive aspect of your solution. You like it, you bastard."

"I'm human, Mr. Cant. Isn't that what you admire? Human frailty?" The corners of the mouth came down in a gargoyle smile.

"What happened to scientific detachment, Doctor?" I wanted to reach up and grab his throat, and I became aware suddenly that I was strapped to the bed.

"I am not totally without emotion, Mr. Cant." Smugness now.

"That, Doctor, is, as the Italians say, where the donkey falls."

"I don't understand that expression."

"You wouldn't. You've got me, Doctor, pinioned to this bed like a roped calf. You can do as you will with my brain, but as sure as there's a God in heaven my soul will live and you'll burn in hell, you demented monster."

I spat into his face.

He sputtered in search for words, then he blew his cool entirely, cursing me at the top of his lungs and beating me with both fists. A nurse and an orderly burst through the door and pulled him off me. He was blue with rage and I laughed at him through the warm blood trickling from my already swelling lips.

15.

"**T**HE court will come to order!" The black-robed judge pounded the gavel on the top of the two-story bench.

"That is my job," said the bailiff, who was all of two hundred feet in height.

"No, it's not!" said the judge in a thundering voice. The bailiff took two giant steps and was at the bench.

"It is!" he shouted. Then he added with a crashing fist to the judge's mouth, "Your Honor."

I ran back of the courtroom and into the arms of a giant woman.

"There, there, Sebby," she said, and produced a handkerchief into which I blew my nose. I looked back, and with horror saw that the judge's head was on upside down.

"Order in the court!" he yelled, and pounded the gavel. "Where did he go, Bailiff?"

"Who, Your Honorable?"

"Not Your Honorable; Your Honor! Your Honor!" the judge screamed and pounded the gavel. White chalk dust flew up from the bench with each blow.

"Make him stop!" I cried, and pressed my tear-streaked face into the woman's breasts.

"Who put the ceiling on the floor?" the judge screamed, and the white dust flew as he crashed the huge mallet down again and again. The bailiff turned from the bench with a disgusted wave of his hand.

"Aw, you're crazy, Judge."

"I am not!" the judge screamed. He stood up to his full height, at least four stories, and pounded and screamed, the white chalk dust enveloping his horrible upside down head. "Put it back; that's an order of the court!"

"Make him stop," I cried, and began pounding the breasts of the large woman. "Make him stop."

"Secure the cozy," a female voice said.

"How did he get his arms free again?" another of the same gender asked.

"Beats me," the first replied, "he's a regular Houdini. And in his sleep, yet."

My eyes opened. It was Kelly Green. Her sweet freckled face was smiling down at me from one side of the bed, while another nurse on the other side was helping her re-entrap me in the cozy. I tightened the muscles of both

arms so that they were immovable. Both
nurses tried in vain to unstraighten them, talking gently, but their grunts betraying that
they were using all their strength. I am quite
strong, and they were unsuccessful. Kelly
Green tried the con approach.

"You're strong all right, Seb." When she
called me Seb, it flashed to mind that I had
made love to this girl and absently I allowed
my muscles to slacken.

"Will you let us put the cozy back on, Seb?"

"No." My arms stiffened again.

"Won't you trust me?" she said softly, with
a hint of hurt feelings in her voice.

"You ask me to trust you to put me in a
contraption that is an obvious display of *your*
mistrust of me. That makes sense." She sat
down beside me on the bed.

"You'll fall out of bed without it. You already have, once."

She looked at her partner and jerked her
head toward the door, and the other nurse responded by leaving the room without a word.

"When are they going to do it, Kelly
Green?"

"Do what?" she said, and her reply sounded
so genuinely innocent that I thought for a
moment she may not have really known what I
was talking about.

"You know," I tested.

"I don't, Seb. Honestly. You were brought in

here suffering seizures as far as I know, and I'm to see that you're comfortable and watch that they don't recur, that's all. What do you suspect? What do you mean by when are they going to do it? Do what?"

She *was* innocent. I should have known that the owner of that freckled face was not possessed of the kind of guile necessary to perform such acting. She was telling the truth. They had no doubt told her that I had had seizures and instructed her to guard me in a friendly and watchful manner. If I could fake them into believing that I thought her part of the conspiracy, I would have an edge on the bastards. Maybe just enough.

"I don't believe you," I said with conviction.

"That hurts, Seb. We haven't been exactly strangers."

"I'll let you put the cozy on if you give me a kiss." I smiled my best charming smile.

"Okay." She grinned back.

She bent over and brought her lips to mine. As she did, I eyeballed the camera at the upper left corner through almost closed lids. I took her head in my hands and pressed her cheek to mine so that my mouth was at her ear and I whispered:

"Please trust me, love. Don't tie the knot on the cozy. Don't. Please."

I pressed her cheek hard against mine in a squeeze that was less intended to express affection than it was to emphasize my urgent desperation.

"Will you put on the cozy now, Seb?" she said lightly, but her eyes stared hard into mine.

"Anything you say, Kelly Green. I trust you." I said with all the meaning in the world.

I allowed her to slip my arms into the medieval leftover, and she drew the canvas straps across me and under the bed. She gave a couple of tugs which tightened me down pretty good, and my heart sank in a sea of despair. She straightened up and sat on the bed.

"There," she said, "that wasn't so bad."

Then, "I've missed you, Seb. When you're well, will you . . ."

She bent down again and kissed me and held my shoulders and pressed her cheek to mine.

"A slip knot," she whispered almost inaudibly. "A hard tug'll undo it."

She straightened up again and got to her feet and walked to the rear of the room out of my field of vision. I strained my head up to see her. She had her back to me and was busy at something on the cabinet in front of her.

"Now I have to give you a little shot," she said, and she turned to face me. She held up a hypodermic in one hand and plunged it into the rubber cap of an inverted bottle held in her other. My mouth and throat went dry.

"What is that, Kelly Green?"

"Just something to make you relax," she said. "Isn't that a stock nurse phrase?"

"Yes," I said, once again in the pit of despair.

She held the hypo and the bottle up to the light as she drew on the syringe. Then she turned her back to me for a minute, and when she again faced me she held a small tray in both hands. Salome, I thought, almost aloud, and turned my head away on the pillow. I heard her place the tray on the bedstand on the other side of me and felt the mattress sag under her weight as she sat on the bed.

She rolled up my sleeve and daubed my upper arm with a wad of alcohol-soaked cotton. I felt the prick of the needle with a resigned disappointment, but then I felt something else that made my spirits soar. The liquid of the syringe ran in a tiny cool rivulet down the back of my arm and I could feel it soaking into the sheet under my ribs. I turned my head to her. She was seated so that her back shielded what she was doing from the eye of the camera, and to further hide it she had the needle head under the wad of cotton that she held against my arm. Beautiful. Gorgeous. Perfect. God bless the instinctive guile of the female.

"That hurt a bit, Kelly."

"That's what they all say," she joked nimbly. She put the hypodermic needle back on the tray, and brought the top sheet up to my chin. "There," she said, tucking the sheet under me and standing up. "You'll have a good night's rest."

In a flash she had gathered up her paraphernalia and was out the door with a last look and a wink that was a wish of good luck.

I lay back on my pillow in the silent room, dark except for some lamplight that seeped through the curtained windows and the thin white glow that sprayed the carpet at the hallway door.

I then made the stupid decision to wait a while before making my move. Between the darkness of the room and the fact that I was momentarily freed of anxiety, I lost the battle and drifted off, fighting sleep even as it drew me under.

16.

THE view was from an operating table straight up to bright floodlights that gave off a glow of heat that warmed my forehead uncomfortably. Each face that loomed over me was surgically masked with a white Styrofoam cup that muzzled the nose and mouth, above which strained concentrating eyes. The cold blue eyes in charge were those of Bananastein, recognizable along with the hard voice that crackled commands to his teammates.

"Sorry, Doctor, the anesthetic doesn't seem to be doing its job. We're experiencing unreasonable activity on a conscious level."

What an odd phrase, I thought.

"Freeze him locally."

"I *am* trying, Doctor," a nurse above me said. "We aren't getting a response."

"Freeze him! I want this patient still if you have to hit him with a pipe wrench!"

With that remark I closed my eyes slowly and held myself quiet.

"Better," said Bananastein to the nurse, "much better."

He turned my head, pressing my right cheek hard against the white laundry-scented sheet, and his strong hands were dreamily reminiscent of my long-forgotten father turning my head to check the cleanliness of my ears after a bath.

"Shave him again," Bananastein ordered disgustedly.

"Yes, Doctor."

Softer, gentler hands pushed my hair against its nap and applied shaving cream to skin that was bare where it shouldn't be. The hairless spot I had seen on John Macky's temple flashed before my eyes, along with the room full of zombies, and the awful traffic light, and I felt the panic sweep through my body, and I was suddenly violently arching my back in terror-charged strain against the restraining straps that pinioned me.

"For God's sake, hold him!" yelled Bananastein, and all hands pressed me to the table. Only my head was free, and I held that up as high as I could, as if I could somehow pull myself free with only my neck muscles.

"Hold still, Sebastian. It's pointless to struggle." he said.

"He's right, Seb." God! It was Julie!

"You bitch! You bitch!" I screamed, but no sound came out of my mouth. Had the inhuman bastards already done something to my voice box? Had they cut or removed my vocal cords? I doubled my fists under the sheet and strained against the straps. Each arm was pinned down at the waist. A strap across my legs just above the knees and another across my chest. I somehow felt I was going to burst them all; that nothing could hold my rage.

"Hold him, you fools! He's strong!" It was Julie now. She had taken charge, it seemed. I strained my head up higher, raising my shoulders off the table, my upper body in a taut arch. I wanted to get my hands on her. To strangle her. To rip out her eyes.

"Syringe," commanded Bananastein, in charge again. A nurse slapped a hypodermic in his open palm.

"Where?" she asked.

"The right eye," he said, and my bowels let go. Incredibly, through the panic I felt an oblique stab of embarrassment that was instantly drowned in overwhelming animal terror.

"No! No!" I screamed, and still no sound came from me. "No!" My body arched the opposite way now. My head twisted to the left. My cheek pressed against the table in an incredible effort to turn my head face down to guard my eyes from that awful needle only inches away.

"Turn his head! Turn his head!"

I sat bolt upright.

Free.

The faces were gone.

The room was dark.

The knot in the cozy had loosed as Kelly Green had promised and I sat up, my arms still folded in the position they were held by the cozy. I was soaked with sweat and the unconcerned, busy voices coming under the door with the hallway light told me I had not cried aloud in my nightmare.

I lay back on the dampened pillow and gathered myself mentally. How much time had passed? I had no way of knowing. A minute? An hour? Two, three? Speculating was pointless. Whatever had put me to sleep, whether it was some drug that was included in my last meal, or the whim or wish of an interested God, my time for moving was on me. If too much time had passed, they might be coming for me right at the moment. They might be turning the corner with their gurney and its restraining straps.

I got out of bed. I was dressed in a hospital gown and nothing else. I padded to the door and holding the stupid gown closed behind me with one hand, I opened the door slowly and carefully to a crack no wider than the breadth of a penny.

The view of the hallway was blurred because

of the tiny aperture and as I pressed close to the crack I widened it carefully by centimeters until the hall fell into focus. It was busier than Grand Central. I let the door close and crept back to bed. How in God's name was I going to get out of the room, much less down the hall to a stairwell? The elevator was out. I couldn't just stand there with my ass hanging out of my gown and wait for the elevator doors to open to reveal who-knows-who standing inside. It had to be the stairs. But where were they? Exit was a dirty word at Sunnyview and there were no arrows bearing the invitation.

Suddenly I heard the voices of two men who had stopped just outside the door.

I giggled. The kind of insane giggle that escapes at funerals. A hand pushed the door open a few inches and the room flooded with light and sound; then as quickly, the hand withdrew and the door shut again.

Two men were engaged in some kind of debate. I couldn't make out the substance of the argument, but whatever it was, it was a blessing. It gave me a minute to think, and I had to think fast. In a moment they would be through the door and there would be no options. None at all.

I slipped out of bed and eased myself into a prone position on the cold floor on the side opposite the door. The light flared a moment as the door opened again and closed. More debate.

Good. I hoped they would talk outside that god-damn door forever. I assumed a push-up position, raising myself on my hands and toes until my arms were straight. Then, pressing my chin to my chest so that my face would strike the floor before any other part of my body, I hesitated a moment for a quick prayer and threw both my hands out and away.

Reflex, which can never be totally controlled, began to raise my forehead up in the split second's drop and I landed full weight on my nose. A stroke of luck. I didn't knock myself out and my nose spewed blood convincingly just as the room filled with light for the third and last time.

"He's gone!"

No I'm not, I prayed. Come around, you meatheads. I'm over here. I fell out of bed.

"Here he is!" an orderly said. "He must have torn himself loose in his sleep and fallen out of bed."

I let myself go dead weight limp as they muscled me back on the bed. The blood flow tickled my nose and throat and I held and prayed against a sneeze.

"You get the gurney, I'll see if I can stem the hemorrhaging."

"Okay, Chuck."

Chuck's partner left the foom for the gurney and Chuck, God bless his well-trained heart, stemmed the hemorrhaging by the expedient

method of pinching my nostrils shut. I couldn't
hold it. The blood gagged me and I threw up.
"Oh shit," was Chuck's sensitive comment.

"What happened?" asked his equally bright
comrade as he bumped a gurney through the
door and muscled it parallel to my bed.

"He threw up," elucidated Chuck.

"Oh. Here," the other said, and a cloth was
wiping my mouth and chin.

They lifted me onto the gurney and I wondered, as they did, whether there would be
straps and whether they would use them. My
luck held. There were straps all right. Two of
them. A leg strap and a chest strap, but they
merely laid them across me without fastening
them. They then bumped and jostled the gurney out the door, and I felt myself rapidly
moving down the hall feet first.

"So?" said Chuck over my head.

"So what?" asked the other.

"So are you going to take Alice tonight and
leave me Mary?"

"Let me think about it."

"Think about it? Come on, man, it's six-
thirty already."

Up to then I couldn't chance opening my
peepers to glimpse a passing clock and I wasn't
dead sure within four hours, so the orderly's
chance remark as to the time was a godsend.
Also, six-thirty put me within an hour of dusk,
so it was a perfect time. All except for the ob-

stacle of getting away from the coconuts who now had me in their charge.

Even with my belief in God, I never could quite swallow the Almighty actually paying attention to the individual to the point of manipulating earthly circumstances. My personal theology had never admitted guardian angels. However, perhaps my punching the devil's disciple, Bananas, in the mouth after proclaiming my allegiance to the other side was so cheered in the rafters that maybe someone was persuaded to move a few stars around that night. What happened next convinced me.

"What the hell is the matter?" asked Chuck.

"I have a charley horse," said the other. The gurney had come to a halt and both voices moved to my left and then to my rear. I was dying to take a peek but restrained the urge.

The chatter became very animated and a nurse joined the two knotheads. The gist of their discussion was whether they should wait for the muscle to relax or whether Chuck should press on, leaving his wounded comrade, and deliver me. The nurse took the helm, suggesting with the appropriate allusions to loyalty that the body delivery was the priority, and with a lurch, Chuck was back on the job and we were rolling again.

A halt. The ting of the elevator bell. A wait. A bumping short roll, the sound of doors closing, and the Otis hummed. It was now or never. I opened my lids to permit a slit of blurred vision. Chuck's back was to me as he faced the elevator buttons and lights. I opened my lids to widen the screen. We were alone in the rising cubicle.

I leaped on his neck. I shut off his wind and his voice with my forearm. I was not adept at the thuggee business, so I rather awkwardly just kept pounding his head against the elevator control board until he went limp and slumped to the floor. The elevator doors opened and I buttoned them shut quickly before two gaping nurses collected themselves.

Small wonder that the nurses were shocked. My gown was smeared with blood from Chuckie's lacerated scalp and a hand to my cheek told me that same was on my face. I must have looked a sight. Anyway, it served a purpose. They didn't board. On impulse I fingered a daub of blood from my gown and deposited it on the lens of the cameras in the upper corners. I then pressed "L.L." and the elevator began descending.

In that eternal hesitation between the moment an elevator stops and doors open, it came to me that they could be already waiting for me in the basement. That they could have somehow perceived my plan. That they saw it in my dreams. In John's brain waves. Somehow, I fancied, they knew, and in the space of those moments I dreamed up a regiment of muscled orderlies waiting for me outside the elevator. It was, therefore, no real shock when there was someone.

She was young. Pretty, as they all were pretty, her big eyes taking in the awful picture in front of her as the doors parted like curtains on a macabre play.

I acted quickly, and if I do say so, with nimble-footed cunning.

"Quickly," I said, "take this man to three! Hurry! They need every hand!" I pulled her into the elevator by her arm, pressed the button for the third floor, and jumped out, standing facing her as the doors closed on our switched positions. "Third floor!" I repeated. "Ceiling caved in on that west wing! Awful! Awful!"

The machine ground upward behind the closed doors, and I held for a few seconds to watch the light above the door indicate it had passed the first floor. Then I kicked off in a dead run for my destination, my bared ass chilled and my open blood-stained gown flapping as my bare feet slap-slapped down the cold corridors.

In seconds I had found my first stop . . . the linen closet. I pushed open the unlocked door and found the janitor's uniform of old khaki fatigues on a hook. My gown came off and in no more than a minute I was into the fatigues and back out the door running again.

Second stop, the men's room. The stall where I had sung "Yes, Sir, That's My Baby", and where I had stashed the key in the crack in the wall. The key. The key that John had mentioned on the golf course before they grabbed him. The key to the monkey room . . . and much more. My hands trembled with fear and physical exertion as I felt for it. It was there! I had it. I had the jewel and I bolted for the door with it tight in my fist.

Now the juices were pumping through me with the exhilaration that is the brother to panic. Not the teeth of the monster closing on my heels but the first toe-touch of bottom in the swim to shore from the dark drowning waters. I felt for the first time that escape from Sunnyview was a possible reality.

As I neared the last corner, I reached out my right hand and pressed my palm, running, against the wall using the friction like a motorcyclist uses a steel-capped heel to round a corner without deceleration. My heart was pumping through my chest when I finally reached, and skidded past, my goal. I plunged my hands into my pockets. Which pocket had the key? I almost tore my pants grabbing for the key that wasn't there. "Oh, God!" I yelled aloud as I heard the elevator doors open and the excited banter of the people it spilled into the cavernous basement. Side pockets. No! Back pockets. No! I could hear them yelling as they spilt their party in two, the better to search the labyrinth. I guessed there were probably a dozen or so of them. Utter despair and resignation overwhelmed me and I felt my stomach begin to spasm. I was going to throw up.

I yanked both my side pant pockets inside out and the key clattered to the floor. Someone fifty or so yards away from the nearby corner yelled, "This way!" in response to the resounding noise of that small piece of metal. Damn the acoustics, I cursed, as I scooped it up. I took a deep breath to steady my shaking hands enough to insert it in the lock, turned it, burst through the door and locked it fast behind me. The din of the simian chorus was music.

I couldn't pause. I had to move very quickly. Once they discovered where I was, the alarm would be sent to cover my escape through the window. I ran to the glass cabinet, opened it, and snatched the transmitter. The cacophony of the chimps increased abruptly, with Elwood leading the bleachers. He shook his cage violently. In seconds I clicked the toggle switch to open the window. It slid into the wall, its metal frame moving on metal tracks in agonizing slow motion. The front door began trembling under the pounding fists and shoulders of the invaders and, impossibly, the volume of the screaming monkeys increased.

I was through the window before it was half

open, clambering up the built-in wall ladder with the transmitter tight in my hand. Outside, passing orderlies and nurses were stopped in their tracks by the sound of the screaming animals that suddenly blared from the fully open window behind me. They were so stunned that they gave no chase or hindrance as I ran past them toward the woods.

The first of the orderlies who pursued me in the basement came through the window after me. They had either successfully broken down the door to the monkey room or produced a duplicate key. Looking over my shoulder as I ran, I pressed the second switch that opened all the cages in the room, and I heard the screams of the people still inside above the voices of the animals.

With the edge of the woods no more than twenty yards away, I looked back to see white uniforms and crazed chimps pouring from the window. I flung myself into the brush that aproned the woods like a surfer plunging into breakers.

I flipped and rolled over, bramble bushes lacerating my face, and knelt, hidden, and watched the show. The expression "monkey on my back" came to mind and hysterical laughter surged in my chest, strangled and made mad by the mortal fear of capture. The scene before me was a bedlam. The simians were crazed with fear and panic compounded by the fear

and panic of the white-frocked orderlies trying
to capture them bare-handed. The cries of the
men mingled with the shrill screeching of the
animals in an olio of sounds orchestrated
louder and louder and rising to the heavens
above the scene like some demonic symphony.

It's appropriate, I thought, as I watched
with dangerous entrancement. It's the hell that
is Sunnyview, defrocked and revealed.

My eyes panned the scene, caught a figure,
and zoomed in on it. It was Manna. Incongruously still amid the rioting.

My God, I thought, he's looking straight at
me. He sees me.

I turned quickly, my feet gouging the earth
under me as, still in a crouch, I ran. Thick foli-
age whipped my face and hands as I ran, my
heart pounding high in my chest, the animal-
panting burning the air into my lungs. I fell. I
got up almost before I hit the ground, my
hands and feet acting autonomously, scram-
bling me erect to run again.

I craved, no, lusted for distance with a
madman's passion.

At last the sounds of Sunnyview were lost to
the distance and I put one foot in front of the
other until my body quit and fell forward and
my bleeding hands and face felt the rich damp
earth of the forest floor.

With a final effort I rolled over onto my back

and stared dully at the ceiling of sky and converging treetops.

A lone blackbird flapped into view and alighted near to the top of one of the pines. With erratic movements of its head, it poked and preened under its wing. Then, answering some command of God or nature or instinct, it sprang from its perch, flitted upward, soared over the treetops, and was gone. My vision blurred as saline tears brimmed over and stung my cut cheeks and I lay there alone in the forest crying in joyful solitude.

I was free.

Preview

KILLSHOT

by Tom Alibrandi

The following pages are excerpts edited from this new novel scheduled for publication in January, 1979.*

Killshot:

more than a game.

Killshot:

When one player, by virtue of perfect execution and precise coordination, drives the handball in such a fashion so it strikes the front wall low to the floor, allowing his opponent no possibility for a return shot.

The Arte of Handball
by S. O'Dwyer
Dublin, Ireland, 1815

But there is a second kind of Killshot:

When a certain breed of renegade player attempts to hit his opponent with such force so as to maim or otherwise injure him . . . for life.

By the time Coldiron and Barry worked their way into the South, they had been on the road for a little over five months. They were also more than $60,000 to the good, and it looked like they had only dipped into the till. The road promised them much more. Everywhere they went, the best handballers wanted a crack at Barry West. His growing reputation was attracting them in flocks.

The kid had been winning more handily than ever. Though his competition had grown keener as they went, and in spite of the grueling schedule Coldiron had been arranging for him, West seemed to be improving weekly. His victories were coming easier.

It had also become evident to Barry that the old man was in some kind of a hurry, like they had to do it all in a certain period of time. The kid was pulling on his gloves at least three times a week. Sometimes as many as five times. His coach seemed obsessed with tearing the country apart behind the abundant talent of Barry West.

If Coldiron hadn't been so driven with arranging Barry's schedule of matches; if he hadn't spent so much time and thought glorying in their growing pile of money; and if he hadn't been so intent on moving up that triangle his mind showed him every night before he passed out from Green, he might've noticed earlier.

Sure, the kid was unbeatable. He was winning big. He was demolishing everyone who Coldiron put him up against. But it was how he had been winning that was to finally become evident to his coach. Barry West had begun hitting people.

At first, Tate hadn't noticed. Once he did, he was sure it was coincidence. It was a game in which the ball travels in excess of one hundred miles an hour; it was a sport in which each player sweated so profusely the ball could easily get away from someone. Accidents could and did happen in handball. Players often got hit with the bullet-like shots. It was considered part of the risk of playing the game. It was regrettable when it did happen, and the man who accidentally hit his opponent felt bad. It just happened sometimes. Sometimes.

It took until Fredericksburg, Virginia, for Coldiron's attention to be drawn to what was happening. It was in a match against Mike Montague that the change in the kid began to come into focus to Coldiron's bleary eyes.

Montague was a year older than West, and was equally as aggressive on the court. He had just driven an alley pass along the left side wall, in an attempt to move Barry out of the center court zone. The shot had gotten away from the Southerner; it was too high, above the shoulders and two feet off the side wall. To be effective, an alley pass needed to be as close to both the floor and side wall as possible. As it was, West was left with an excellent opportunity for a rollout kill. He was in good position and the ball hung in the air like a ripe apple. The dozen or so people in the gallery, Coldiron, and even Montague himself figured West would easily put it away.

Only the kid didn't go for the rollout. He exploded out of the rear corner, catching his opponent's hard drive in its full momentum, and proceeded to drop Montague with a vicious shot to the back of the neck.

Montague was unconscious on the floor. Coldiron stood in shocked concern with the others in the gallery. He wondered if the others had seen what he had. Montague hadn't even been in the kid's shot-line to the front wall. It appeared ˙at West had deliberately hit his opponent, like he had ꞁed the guy up in a rifle scope. Tate hoped his eyes had ꞁd.

The place was quiet as Montague's second held a vial of ꞁmelling salts to the fallen man's face. The player's head jerked. His neck spasmed around the area where he had been struck by the ball. He came out of it, but not before his stomach had its say. Montague vomited on the man bent over him; it was the involuntary reflex that sometimes accompanies a deadening blow to the base of the skull. The stricken man was helped to his feet, and walked unsteadily, holding on to his attendant.

Coldiron shifted his attention to West. What he saw sent a chill through him. He was looking at a face without remorse. It was the face of a man without shock. It was the look of someone who had just completed a mission.

Montague was done. He had been hit in such a way that the energy had left him like the air being let out of a balloon. West had nailed him in one of the spots. Mike Montague was unable to continue within the fifteen-minute forfeiture time allowance. West had won the match in the first game. He had barely broken a sweat.

Coldiron waited until they were packing their car to leave to talk with West.

"You got off easy today. Too bad about that kid getting hit."

"Yeh. I felt real bad. He's okay, though. Lucky he was only shaken up."

"Yeh. Real lucky. What happened down there? Didn't you see him when you teed off?"

"No. The guy jumped in front of me after I had already pulled the trigger. There was nothing I could do. I really hated to see it happen."

"Right, kid. Those things are a bitch. Sometimes a guy just seems to jump in front of your shot. I know how it goes."

"That's what happened. Montague seemed to just jump in front of me at the last second.

"Where to next, Tate?"

"South. Way South," Coldiron said and climbed into the passenger side of the car. He'd try to forget what happened in Fredericksburg. He really wanted to believe the kid.

That night Coldiron tried to shut off his mind with Green. His thoughts made it through the alcoholic haze. He lay in bed and tried to answer the questions that sliced at him. The same ones came at him. Over and over.

Why was Barry doing it? The kid had more talent than seven guys. Maybe Fredericksburg was an accident? Maybe the way Montague got hit, looking like he was set up, was just imagination?

As the questions were the same, so were his answers to them. Barry had started hitting people on purpose. There was no mistaking that. Fredericksburg had only turned his mind to it, allowed Coldiron to add it all up.

An occasional hit could easily be an accident. Even a couple of them. But Barry had picked off seven people in the last month. That was more than coincidence. Especially with a player of West's caliber. The kid could put an egg in a china cup at fifty feet, without breaking either. Barry West could put that hard rubber ball anywhere he wanted.

Which is what Coldiron knew he had been doing. West was sticking people in the spots; he was hitting them in the right places to slow them down, force them into losing their concentration or, as in Montague's case, into forfeiting the match to him. What was especially frightening to Tate was that the kid had the skill and power to cripple a man. Even kill him. Coldiron had showed him how.

Tate was wracked with indecision. It was making him crazy. Should he confront the kid? Lay his cards on the table? Let West know he was heading for big danger? Then what? What if he did? What if West told him to shove it and walked? What if he ended the partnership and went on without Coldiron? The kid could make it without Tate. But Coldiron knew he sure as hell couldn't make it without the kid. And he was so damn close.

Barry's next match destroyed any doubts Coldiron might've had that the kid was hitting people on purpose. It happened in the third and match-deciding game. West had his hands full with Corley Stinson. His dark-haired and handsome opponent was playing an extremely skillful game of handball. Midway through the third game he hit Stinson. West was trailing 10-11 at the time. He was running out of gas when he paralyzed Stinson with a bullet to the groin. The Southern man's scream had hardly stopped rebounding from the stark walls when it was discovered that his left genital had been shattered. He was still writhing on the floor when the ambulance attendants wheeled the gurney into the court. The match was over.

Tate walked back to the hotel. His legs were killing him. The pain in his heart was even greater. He had to have time to think. Coldiron had a killer on his hands. The kid would stop at nothing to win.

Even winning was no longer enough. The kid was addicted to the thought of becoming the best in the game. He had tasted the sweetness of fame. He was a top gun. They were lining up to take a crack at him. Lining up to play a hitter who liked the taste of blood.

One part of Coldiron knew clearly what he must do. The kid had to be dealt with before he killed somebody. Another part of the old fox refused to accept the obvious. Tate had been a loser for twenty-five years, clawing for crumbs. That made it easy to deny, not that the kid was a hitter, that West had to be dealt with. A very convincing voice in him said the kid would turn it around before it got too far.

Fear helped Tate consider that Barry would stop hitting people. Maybe if he lightened up on the kid's schedule, so West could get more rest, more time to let off steam. Maybe if Barry were less pressured and frantic he would go back to playing honest fourwall. Maybe it wasn't too late. Maybe the obsession to be the best wasn't too great. Maybe the taste of blood wasn't too strong in the kid's mouth. Maybe those who voted to take out the hitters hadn't yet noticed. Maybe he could forget the whole thing. Maybe.

There was the triangle. And the appointment Tate had promised himself he'd keep that night in the alley in New Orleans. Coldiron was gripped with his own obsession. It was every bit as strong as Barry's compulsion to win.

In the final analysis he knew it was only a matter of time. He could only push it down so far with Jack Daniel's Green. The inevitable could be postponed for only so long. Coldiron's prayer was that his own compulsion and the Green could dull his conscience long enough until he could hobble up what was left of that triangle. He had to keep that appointment.